MEET THE FORCE RECON TEAM . . .

JACK SWAYNE

The leader of the team. A brilliant tactician and superb soldier. For him, failure is not an option . . . ever.

GREINER

The Boy Scout. In the infantry battalion he won Marine of the Month—every month. And he's all too ready to test his mettle in the field.

NIGHT RUNNER

A full-blooded American Indian. Even with the cutting-edge technology used by the team, the deadliest thing about him is his senses.

FRIEL

An ex–street thug turned disciplined Marine. A natural-born killer with no remorse. Possibly the deadliest shot in the world.

FORCE RECON

The explosive military action series by
James V. Smith, Jr.

FORCE RECON

DEEP STRIKE

JAMES V. SMITH, JR.

BERKLEY BOOKS, NEW YORK

This is a work of fiction. Names, characters, places, and incidents either are the product of the author's imagination or are used fictitiously, and any resemblance to actual persons, living or dead, business establishments, events, or locales is entirely coincidental.

FORCE RECON: DEEP STRIKE

A Berkley Book / published by arrangement with the author

PRINTING HISTORY
Berkley edition / November 2002

Copyright © 2002 by James V. Smith, Jr.

Visit our website at
www.penguinputnam.com

ISBN: 0-425-18709-8

BERKLEY®
Berkley Books are published by The Berkley Publishing Group,
a division of Penguin Putnam Inc.,
375 Hudson Street, New York, New York 10014.
BERKLEY and the "B" design
are trademarks belonging to Penguin Putnam Inc.

PRINTED IN THE UNITED STATES OF AMERICA

10 9 8 7 6 5 4 3 2 1

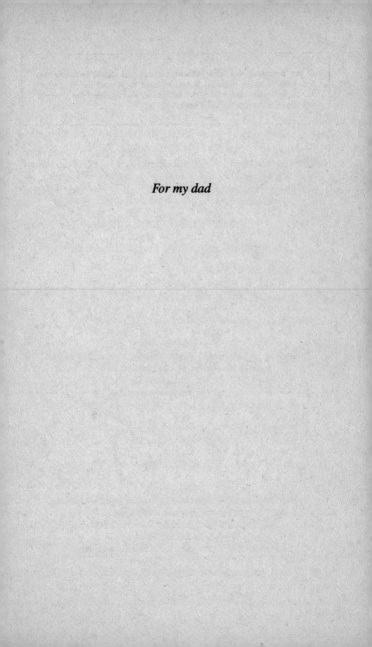

For my dad

EVENT SCENARIO 18

"CONDOR." NIGHT RUNNER'S one-word signal spoke volumes to each member of Force Recon Team 2400.

To Gunnery Sergeant Robert Night Runner, the Blackfeet warrior turned Marine Corps warrior, it was a simple report, no more, no less. He had left the other three members of the team in a secure assembly area so he could make his recon. He had drifted across the desert floor like a black fog, silent and invisible in the night.

He had become one with the night, the dense, chill air an offshoot of his awareness, his thinking, his blood. He was more a spirit than a man. More lethal than nerve gas. More lethal than even that most deadly of killing machines, the Force Recon Marine. He was, at times like this, Death itself.

He took his direction from the stars rather than the GPS in his pocket. He measured his distance in paces, feeling the ground through the thin, flexible soles of his boots. He liked the feel of Mother Earth. He had designed the boots himself. Dyed buckskin uppers hugged his ankles and calves like camouflaged stockings. Soft rubber, thinner and with more grip than rock-climbing shoes, clung to the bottom of his feet. Space-age mocs, he called them.

Friel had laughed at first sight of them. "Why not just spray-paint freakin' camo on your bare feet?"

Night Runner had only raised an eyebrow in answer. Why not indeed? He had devoted himself to the training regimen of a true Blackfeet a year ago. He had gone into the wild areas of the country, from Montana to California to Texas, just as Friel had suggested. In bare feet. With no weapons. With no tools. With no clothes—except for a bathing suit, his only concession to civilization, and then only out of concern for others. The few people who might spot him at all would not see him as a warrior in training. They would see only a naked, crazy man.

So he would have been at ease in bare feet. His soles were tough as leather. Here in Iran he was testing the boots in the hope that he might train his men and his officer to use them. If he could find a way to make the Marines of Team Midnight more silent, he could make them even more deadly. They would never be able to achieve his degree of stealth because only he had the blood for it. He was one pure hunter and fighter in a long line of generations of hunters and fighters who had crossed the land bridge from Asia in prehistory. They had come in bare feet. Or at best, with their feet wrapped in the skins of seals and bears.

Whereas the white man had come from generations of people with soft feet covered by hard soles. Their boots had trod the ground without ever allowing their feet to get the feel of earth.

But they could do better than stumble across hostile landscapes like drunks on stilts. If they would only let themselves be trained out of their whiteness a little. Even more, Night Runner wished he could train Friel out of the sickness of heart that had infected him for months. A sickness that had been poisoning the man's spirit for weeks. A poison that had become toxic to other members of the team for days. A toxicity that had become a situation. A negative situation.

But a negative he could not solve tonight. Tonight the team—his team—had a mission. Maybe a mission, even one as bland as theirs, could be used to heal.

After he uttered *Condor* into the boom mike at his lips, he went back to his study of the scene a half mile away. As CIA analysts had said, a low-grade terrorist training area lay before him. A dozen wooden frames in all. Canvas had been stretched over half the frames. A sparse web of netting had been laid over that, a feeble attempt to hide the structures from spy drones and satellites.

From the arrangement he could guess how the camp was manned. Three frames were side by side, each with a slit-trench latrine a hundred meters out behind. A hitching post let men belly up to urinate. Or hold onto it while leaning backward over the trenches to relieve themselves. The post also kept the night wanderer from stepping into the trench.

So Night Runner knew those buildings were barracks.

A fourth building nearby would be the mess hall. Next, a classroom. Then a headquarters.

A single ring of razor wire circled the camp. Again, a lame effort. Bad enough that it was only a single spiral of wire—an attacker would not even have to throw a plank across the curls to press them down, let alone set up bangalore torpedoes to blow the wire. Any soldier worthy of the name could hurdle it. Except he wouldn't need to. The wire was strung so close to the buildings that a squad of men with pistols could line up outside the wire, sound a wake-up call, and wipe out the camp just by shooting through the walls as men sat up in bed.

All this Night Runner saw without using the night-

vision goggles hanging on a strap around his neck. He
turned his head left and right listening for sounds from
the camp's security force. He heard the rasp of men's
breathing, the closest about fifty meters away. He listened
harder. Two men, both snoring.

He shook his head. Wiping out the camp was their mission. A strike mission, the captain had called it. Now
Night Runner saw why Swayne had given his mission
briefing with so little energy. This camp was no hotbed
of active terrorists. This was no staging area for an attack
on Free World targets.

These were play terrorists. At best this was a part-time
training camp so local weekend martyrs could work off
their fervor without actually harming anybody. Or getting
harmed. The National Guard of martyrdom. Except it was
a National Guard that would never be called up. Just a
place to let would-be zealots work through their inept hostility.

Night Runner looked over the camp through night-
vision binoculars capable of 50-power digital magnification. He saw beer cans in the trash. Old Milwaukee. At
least they had good taste. Leave it to terrorists to be im-
porting beer from the land of the Great Satan in the middle of a trade embargo and drinking it in violation of the
laws of Islam. He switched the binoculars to infrared, and
saw a huge hot spot in the middle of the camp where a
bonfire had raged earlier in the evening. Bones and more
beer cans littered the area.

The so-called terrorists had enjoyed a feast of three
roasted goats—confirmed by satellite photographs—
washed down by gallons of brew. They had not been worried about satellite surveillance by night any more than
by day. Even the Iranians knew they were amateurs—
more a terrorist book club than a terrorist outfit. The Great
Satan would not waste a long-range missile on them, especially if they sat belching and farting in the open, show-

ing that they had nothing to hide, proving they were not a force to fear, neither devout Muslims nor serious terrorists.

Night Runner wondered. Why risk a valuable team of special-operations pros, the best in the business, a Force Recon team? Let alone the Spartans, the best of the best, on this ragtag outfit.

To use one of Friel's words, *shit.*

Night Runner spat between his two front teeth. The Great Satan had indeed risked a Force Recon team of Marines, any one of whom might catch a stray bullet in the think tank. And for what? To hit a toga party of harmless fraternity brothers? To take out a gang of misfits that real terrorists would not even let into their band? To kill—

Night Runner spat again. His job was not to rate the worth of the mission. All that had already been done at a much higher pay grade than his own. He was to think within his own pay grade. He was to recon. Set up the ambush. Strike, hit, kill. No thinking to it, Gunny, just do it. Just kill the play terrorists in retaliation for the deeds of others.

The heat seeped away from his body and mind. His thinking grew cold.

He began unpacking the tools of his trade, feeling the stabbing of pains across his back, reminders that he was a warrior, no more, no less. Night Runner's job was to do so others might die. Let the captain worry about the ethics of the strike.

CAPTAIN JACK SWAYNE cursed under his breath. Never before had he let himself wish for a mission plan to go south. He had hated this operation from the start. From the moment he had been given his mission in the form of a five-paragraph field order.

Everybody in uniform called it the five-paragraph field order. Everybody from the Commandant of the Marine

Corps on down to a Force Recon team leader in Iran used the same format. The Commandant might use a battalion of staff officers to develop his plan into a ninety-eight-page document that only a staff-college grad could decipher. While the team leader might give his order verbally under fire, scratching marks in the sand like kids drawing up a play in touch football. Either order would have the same five paragraphs: Situation, Mission, Execution, Administration/Logistics, and Command and Signal.

Swayne's reputation as a Force Recon Team leader had been made on his ability to think under fire. The same five nails of military logic had always anchored his thinking. He ran through them one at a time.

Paragraph One: Situation. The acronym for covering all the bases in this paragraph was WETT, for weather, enemy, troops, and terrain. Nothing had changed in the weather since his first briefing to the team on the plane en route to their LALO drop with low-altitude, low-opening parachutes.

The troop situation—his own men—remained the same. The entire team of four was intact. Nobody had turned an ankle. Nobody had made what Friel called a SLOB touchdown in polite company—Spinal Landing on Boulders—or a CUTE touchdown when he was among friends, although he had none—Cactus Up The Enus.

Everybody had stayed healthy.

Swayne shook his head. Truth be told, the team was not all that healthy. Nothing on this team was the same as it used to be. Something important had changed to infect the group of four with a touch of disease. Their feeling of invulnerability had eroded.

Team 2400 had lost a man on each of its last two outings. Gunny Potts and Private Perfect. Once again, Swayne and the team had to work with a new guy. So the friendly troop situation would not be settled until they saw how Greiner acted under fire. Swayne bit his lip.

Perfect had come apart, had nearly shot and killed Night Runner, the body and spirit of this team. Swayne knew he might take credit for being the brains of the outfit, but Night Runner was everything else and the reason Team Midnight had had such success over the years. Perfect had panicked. He'd tried to kill the gunny when he was most vulnerable, sprinting back into the team's position while under enemy fire.

Swayne shrugged. No point in hashing that one over again. Perfect would not have been on this mission in any case. Swayne had already made up his mind to remove him from the roster once they returned. That he had died in action—ironically, killed by semi-friendly troops—did nothing more than take the decision out of his hands. Time now to get it out of his head.

Next item in the Situation paragraph: terrain. No change. Everything had turned out exactly as briefed in maps and photographs and video intelligence reports. The video was a new wrinkle in Force Recon operations. Teams in the field could have video transmitted to them from the most up-to-date, most specialized intelligence centers in the world. Information did not have to be diluted by the layer after layer of opinion from intelligence officers at every level. An analyst could show photographs at a target zone, nearly in real time. High-tech software converted photographs into topographic maps that were just minutes old instead of years old, as the conventional troops had to use. If a windstorm had changed the lay of the land overnight, the team in the field would know the location of every new sand dune and could adjust to it. If enemy troops had dug a new slit trench latrine that might cause a broken leg or a terminal case of stinky boot, the analyst could tell them.

Swayne reloaded the map on his screen for the tenth time in the last hour and saw that little had changed, including the analyst's notes typed at the bottom of the screen. He could see that the bonfire had burned out. The coal pit had shrunk in size and intensity as it cooled at its edges.

That left only one thing to consider in the Situation paragraph of the field order. The enemy. Swayne wished that part of the situation would have changed. If only the video had portrayed a different picture. If Night Runner had not uttered the word *Condor*. If the would-be terrorists had only loaded onto a truck convoy and gone home to their mothers, he wouldn't have to kill them.

But they had not. Night Runner had said the word that meant the enemy still sat in the kill zone.

That the code word began with the letter C meant that the team had not been spotted, that the enemy force was no threat to the team, that they could be surprised.

Swayne checked his video, reloading the screen with an infrared image. The overhead infrared sensor highlighted every outpost where a pair of warm bodies huddled together against the chill of the desert night air—and probably slept. These outposts were to provide the camp's only security. Which was no security at all. He counted bodies—and yes, he thought of them as bodies, corpses really, for soon they would be just that.

Twenty to thirty men in each barracks, he guessed. Infrared could not penetrate the canvas and show a hot spot for each person. But the overall heat signature of body heat radiating through the tents on each frame told Swayne the barracks were nearly full of men who had been partying only hours earlier. The men would have to die. Their fate had been decided in the mission given to the Force Recon team. All that remained was for the gates of heaven and hell to open and slam shut on a new batch of immigrants.

"Move out," he murmured into his mike. He didn't need to say another word. They had rehearsed every step already. At a top-secret desert training base in Nevada. A bomb-range impact area. The live ammunition kept the curious away and lent an air of realism to the rehearsal.

He saw the black silhouette of the new kid, Greiner, stand up and begin moving toward Friel's position. A natural reaction to the urgency in his order. But a wrong move. He would have to talk to the kid about it. Remind him—

FRIEL'S VOICE JUMPED into Swayne's ears to remind the kid first.

"How many times the captain got to tell you not to bounce up like a jumping jack and start giving away the position?" Friel said, transmitting not only to Greiner but also the team. As well as to the underground command center at Quantico on the other side of the world. "You give the area the big three-six-zero first, remember? Check out the area? Left? Right? Six? What do you got, Grinder, shit for brains?"

"Yes, sir, Sergeant Friel. I mean, no, sir."

"Shit-fire, Grinder. Make up your mind," Sergeant Henry Friel snarled as he stepped out into the night in the direction Night Runner had disappeared.

"Yes, sir, check the area first, sir, before moving out. And no, sir, Sergeant, I do not have shit—"

"Shut up, Grinder."

Friel didn't much care whether the captain heard him or not. Check that. He wanted the man to know he was pissed. The best shooter in the Marine Corps should not be left in the rear baby-sitting another shit-green, pansy-ass, snot-nosed, slack-jawed, mouth-breathing, knuckle-dragging, freaking new guy. He ought to be up front backing up the gunny. Instead of leaving his ass to hang out. Didn't Swayne remember him having to bail out his butt in Kosovo last mission?

Officers. Only time they remembered something was

when you accidentally shit in their mess kits. Then they couldn't forget it. Never.

Friel clapped a pair of high-tech night-vision binoculars to his face and turned slowly. He swept with his eyes from the near distance to the horizon until he had made a complete circle. At every point of the compass, he stopped to mutter a cuss word to remind himself and the team how pissed off he was.

The night-vision device was the size and shape of single-lens, full-face ski goggles. Not much heavier, either, with all the recent improvements in processing power of computer chips and high-impact graphite. He did not have to look through the lenses of the goggles. Instead, images were collected by four synchro-cameras around the rim, and processed by a series of parallel computers cemented to the back of his helmet in a shell the size and shape of half a grapefruit. The computer array projected an image onto the inside of the goggles lens like a true heads-up virtual-reality display.

Except that it was nearly actual reality. Previous night-vision devices could display pictures of the battlefield. But they were one-dimensional. Walking, driving—and especially flying—were dangerous. A man could look down and see the ground at his feet—and even see his boots as well—but could not tell whether the terrain sloped. Friel had always felt detached from his own feet when he tried to move around with night-vision goggles.

As Night Runner was always bitching, Friel wasn't all that sneaky on a bright night. Add those old goggles, and he got around like one of those Irish-jig dancers who'd been too busy French-kissing an Irish jug.

These were different. Two tiny cameras inside the goggles measured the angle of Friel's eyes as they focused. On near objects, his eyes would cross more than when he looked at distant objects. The cameras would relay every change in focus through the computer back to a pair of

lenses, one on each side of the goggles looking outward.
These would swivel to match the focus of Friel's eyes and
give him true binocular vision at any distance. With a
delay so short, Friel could not detect it.

The larger pair of lenses collected ambient light. A
smaller pair read thermal returns. So the goggles gave
members of Force Recon the dual capability of visual imagery and thermal besides.

"So what?" Friel had asked the first time a CIA tech
briefed him on the NVGs. "That's all bells and whistles.
You can't name me one good use for white light and IR
in the field at the same time."

In fact, the tech had named half-a-dozen ways—
applications, he called them—to use the dual-imagery feature.

"These goggles can be used as range finders," the techie
had said with a sniff. "They have GPS readout capability,
can identify the location of the wearer and instantaneously
report global coordinates of the spot where the operator's
eyes are focused. They're good for firing artillery and directing air strikes without using a laser-guided capability
that could conceivably give away the position. They are,
in short, Mr. Friel, the state of the state of the art."

Friel, never lacking a comeback, had simply stuck out
his shoulder. "See them sergeant stripes?" he'd hissed. "I
ain't a freakin' *mister,* asshole."

"Just a regular asshole then?" the tech had shot back.

Night Runner had had to intercept Friel in mid-lunge.

Now Friel, having checked his position and found it
safe, stood up and began putting one of those state-of-the-
art uses into play.

Friel began following the "bread crumbs" that Night
Runner had dropped along his recon route. A high-level
lab—the toy store, as he called it—was always creating
high-tech devices for spies and special-operations units.
Friel, who was always afraid of getting lost in situations

where he did not have a GPS, had asked for something that would allow him to follow a track of somebody like Night Runner, who never got lost. So the toy store developed thermal bread crumbs. They looked like pebbles the size of a small fingernail. They could be matched to the geology of the area where any mission might occur, although plain gray seemed to do well in any part of the world. Each pebble was impregnated with a dose of low-grade radioactivity. Each gave off the same amount of brightness as the luminous dial of a wristwatch. Except that the emission was in the infrared range rather than the visual range of frequencies.

So Friel could watch his footing and check out the landscape using the starlight capability of his goggles. The IR capability picked up the green glow of pebbles Night Runner had dropped to mark his path.

Friel moved quickly. He could have run if he wanted, but then he had detailed Grinder to pick up the bread crumbs along the way. The captain would have his ass if he left the new guy behind.

Forget the freakin' new guy, Friel thought. He had to get up front, had to be ready to lay down some heavy fire support if the chief got into a bind as he set up the ambush. Had to get ready to kick some terrorist ass. Send some ragheads to raghead heaven.

He adjusted his helmet. That was another thing, the helmet. Force Reconners didn't wear helmets—grunts wore helmets. Except that the new goggles required a power pack. It couldn't fit on a cap. So the bonehead scientists had glued it to the back of the helmet like a goiter.

Screw the scientists. Screw the helmet. Screw the new guy. Screw the captain too, if he couldn't get with the program. Things didn't start looking up, and pretty damned quick, Friel was going to say screw the Marine Corps too. Might as well be in the baby-blue Air Force.

• • •

SOMEDAY SOON, SWAYNE decided, he would have to get to the bottom of Friel's attitude. The kid from Boston had always been a smart aleck. On the last two missions, he had developed a nasty edge, a way of stepping over the line that went beyond mere arrogance. He had become borderline insubordinate. Swayne blamed himself. He had been too easy on the man after Potts's death.

Potts had given his own life to save Friel's, and a combination of grief and guilt had been eating at Friel ever since. Then too, there had been Friel's serious wounds. So Swayne had cut him some slack. On the last mission Friel had disobeyed orders. Because that disobedience had led to the shooting that saved the lives of both Swayne and Night Runner, Swayne had done little more than chew him out in the debriefing. A wink and a knock on wood, he had thought. A word to the wiseass. A slap on the backpack. It should have been enough.

It was not. Hell, Swayne had known it would not be.

Rather than take it to heart, Friel had let it go to his headstrong head. He was not the type to profit from a word to the wise. If you gave him slack, he would take it up and play you for more. He was going to get ever more difficult until Swayne jerked his reins. Swayne bit his lip and nodded as he followed his men. It had to be done. Right after this mission.

The mission. That was the next paragraph of the five-paragraph field order. Much as he did not like it, Swayne could not argue with the literal mission statement as it had come down to him from the one-eyed Colonel Zavello. It left no wiggle room. No politician could parse it to pieces. It was too direct, even for lawyers: *Attack and destroy Objective Normandy at H-hour, D-day, neutralizing the enemy's ability to conduct terrorist activities by inflicting maximum casualties on personnel, maximum de-*

struction of fixed facilities, and total destruction of weapons, matériel, and equipment.

"And by the way," Zavello had said, "get your ass out of the country without being detected and without leaving a clue as to your country of origin."

Of course, the mission statement was merely an operations plan until it had a commander's approval to execute. Then somebody filled in the actual time and date for H-hour and D-day.

Swayne checked his watch. H-hour was to be 0330 hours, just eleven minutes away on this D-day for hitting Objective Normandy. He snickered to himself. Objective Normandy indeed. Force Recon teams in other parts of the world would be hitting terrorist Objectives Overlord, Omaha, and Utah at the same time his team would take down Normandy. A nice piece of grand overstatement. Naming a handful of two-bit operations after the Normandy invasion of World War II did not lend any majesty to the mayhem his team was about to unleash.

Still, he could not stop his mind from doing its job. His mind was what elevated him among Force Recon team leaders. He wasn't smarter than anybody else. He had mastered the art of keeping his options open, constantly adapting to the combat situation. Here, he did not expect very much combat. He did not expect the nation to gain very much, no matter how well the team accomplished its mission. For the unspoken part in the second paragraph of the five-paragraph field order was really not that he get his team out without being identified by the enemy. No, in fact, his country *wanted* the terrorists to know who had been there. Where other Force Recon teams would be striking too: Afghanistan, Iraq, Libya, and Romania.

State-sponsored terrorists had propelled an explosive-laden launch into the side of the U.S.S. *Cole,* killing seventeen sailors. Those deaths had outraged a nation. Four other deaths had outraged the Marine Corps. A Force Recon team that could not be acknowledged had been below-decks. They were to have gone over the side at nightfall to engage the very terrorists who had killed them. Now the Marine Corps, in the name of the country, was getting even by striking at known terrorist camps around the world. Sending a message. Or as Zavello put it: "You are going to be sending a message right up their terrorist asses, Captain Swayne. So you'd better hit them hard. Understand?"

Of course Swayne understood. If you took away the revenge aspect of the attack, the mission still had value. The sending-the-message thing. For his team, it would be a mission where Friel's bad attitude, bad as it was, would not likely get them into trouble. Better yet Swayne could take the measure of the new guy, Greiner.

SERGEANT NATHANIEL DAVID Greiner knew that he would, at last, get into the action. The word *Condor* guaranteed action. Battle action. Combat. The one thing on earth that nobody could reliably tell you about. The one true thing that told you something about yourself.

He had to know things about himself. He had passed all the tests so far. His drill sergeants had told him he had earned the right to be called a Marine.

Maybe so. He had completed boot camp, sure. Then again, didn't most everybody? He had walked away with the training company's top honors in marksmanship and physical fitness. So what? Dozens of Marines did that every year. It wasn't enough.

So he had gone to an infantry battalion and earned every promotion he could ahead of time. He had won the battalion's Marine of the Month award so many months in a row that his gunnery sergeant told him the unit was not allowed to recommend him anymore. They wanted other Marines to be honored. *Good for the morale*. That didn't stop the gunny from recommending him for Marine of the Year. Greiner won that one too. They said he had earned it.

Maybe so. Greiner was still not all that impressed with himself. He had the title, the plaque, the certificate, the savings bond, the furlough, the parking spot at the base exchange.

Big deal.

Those things told others he could spit-shine a pair of shoes and polish some brass. He could answer technical questions about ballistics, rifles, patrolling, the Code of Conduct. So what?

He had mastered military trivia was all. If they ever put that on *Who Wants to Be a Marine Millionaire?*, he could go on and use all the tidbits he had crammed into his head and get rich.

It wasn't enough. He wanted to know things about life. Not just any life, but life on the battlefield. Even if that life meant death.

Of course, he hadn't factored Friel into the equation. Friel was something else. Something odd. He had a way of making you feel odd too. You looked into his eyes and saw clear to the dark edge of humanity. You felt the evil infecting your soul, evil shot from Friel's eyes into your own.

He didn't like Friel. Far as he knew, nobody did. Other Force Recon Marines had called him rude, arrogant, crazy, psycho. All true, Greiner supposed. Reasons enough to dislike a man, any man. But that wasn't what made Greiner dislike Friel. He didn't like him for what he saw in his soul, the mirror that made him feel the evil in himself. He couldn't make sense of the contradiction in the idea of being an evil Marine. Damn Friel, making him feel that way.

He had seen the man shoot, though. He had seen so many targets go down so fast that he'd thought the captain and the gunny were playing tricks on him. He'd thought that all three of them had been shooting silhouettes at once. Screwing with the new guy's mind. But no, it had been only Friel. Only Friel—

Greiner's night-vision goggles went black as his head rammed into something. Something soft. He put up his hands and felt Friel's combat pack.

"What are you doing, Grinder?" Friel barked.

"Sorry, Sergeant, sir." His nose hurt and began to leak.

"Stop calling me sir. I ain't no freaking officer. I gotta work for a freaking living."

"Yes, sir—I mean, Sergeant."

"Get into position."

Greiner saw that Friel was pointing. But straight up into the air.

"Over there. Get moving, Marine."

Greiner realized that his goggles had been knocked askew, so the camera lenses collected images like a video camera laid on its side. He adjusted the goggles well enough to see where Friel pointed. He recognized the array of rocks that the captain had picked for him from the spy satellite pictures. But when he tried to walk toward the stack of boulders, he got dizzy, stumbled, and fell over on his side.

"Shithead."

Friel never let up. That was another thing Greiner hated. "You got to calibrate, moron." Again, over the radio.

Greiner felt his skin prickle with embarrassment. He was glad for the night.

He tried to crawl toward the rocks. Instead of coming closer to them, the stones moved laterally in his vision. The goggles wouldn't work unless he took time to calibrate them, he realized. Just as Friel had said.

He felt a sharp pain in first his knee, then the sole of his boot. Friel had kicked his foot, driving the knee into a rock. He kept crawling to get clear of the crazy sergeant.

Yes, it made him angry to be treated like this. But he was
a Force Recon Marine. The discipline he had developed
in training could not be undone in a moment of shame.
Besides, he was getting only what he deserved. No enemy
would be so gentle with him. Still, he was glad for the
darkness, glad that the gunny and the captain could not
see. They were busy in other areas of the objective. They
were doing their jobs. Time he got squared away so he
could do his.

First, calibrate. Greiner wrapped the forefingers and
thumbs of both hands around his NVG frames. With one
finger, he found the dimmer switch that cut down the light
of the projected image. Then he made the goggles fit his
face. He picked out the boulders where he was to set up
a primary position and recon routes back to alternate positions. Looking through the lenses of the goggles, he
could see an outline of one rock lit up by the faint light
of a cluster of stars. He adjusted the camera lenses on the
left side of his goggles first, using a toggle switch to lay
the faint image of the boulder over his actual view of it,
trying to ignore the whiteout caused by the stars. With a
second toggle switch, he overlaid the faint images projected by the right cameras.

He released the dimmer switch, picked up his rifle, and
made ready to hustle into position.

Don't be in too great a hurry to lose your head. He
remembered Night Runner's words. He reminded himself
that he could not let a psycho like Friel rush him into
doing stupid things. Before moving, he scanned near and
far to make sure no enemy had spotted him. First to the
left. Then to the right. Next, to the rear, where he saw
Friel, leg cocked, waiting for an excuse to kick him again.

Finally, he checked ahead, to make sure no enemy
could spot him on the way to his position. Once the way
was clear, he crept to the boulders.

As he slid to his knees behind the stones, he crossed

his eyes and gazed at the digital time that appeared in the window of his heads-up display. Less than ten minutes until H-hour. The digit of the countdown window in the display showed nine minutes, twenty-seven seconds, to be exact.

Greiner wanted to race through the checklist that he had memorized. He remembered Night Runner's words, though, and kept his head.

First, he made a scan of the area again, to make sure that his new position would not reveal him to the enemy. It looked every bit as secure as Captain Swayne had briefed. No threat. No fault that would jeopardize another member of the team.

Second, he looked for the three alternate positions assigned to him. That Captain. He was good. One position to his left, just as the man had said. Two positions to his right. Both good. He checked behind him to make sure he could back away from the rocks without being shot at by the enemy, and come up in a new position, firing to support the team. Make the enemy seem like he was more than one soldier. Never stay in one position long enough to let the enemy draw a bead or bring down mortar fire.

Third, he looked for his mates. Friel was to his left, just now sliding out of sight behind a hillock. Just as well. They could cover each other with fire without seeing each other. They both could support the gunny if he got into trouble—which was their primary mission for now. Best of all, Greiner would not have to look at Friel anymore—or be looked at. The captain would be to his right. He was to signal at the nine-minute mark.

There! Three brief flashes aimed at him through the captain's scope. He picked up thermal return in his goggles, and pumped his fist at the sky three times to acknowledge the signal, knowing the captain would be watching him, expecting him to respond. *Good boy,*

Greiner, good boy. At least he hadn't screwed up in the captain's eyes.

Next, he was to find Night Runner. Find him and cover his movements by fire. He began sweeping the camp methodically with his NVGs. At intervals, he locked into a spot and just stared, looking for a movement. The gunny had taught him that. But with a smile on his face. Night Runner had been daring Greiner to spot him. Greiner had shrugged at the time. What could be so hard about spotting a guy creeping around the desert? Sure, it was night, but he had the best night-vision goggles in the world, with both visual and thermal capabilities. A no-brainer.

Friel and Swayne had both smiled at his reaction. As if nobody could spot the gunny. Maybe not visually. So what? The goggles also had the GPS receiver in the dome on his helmet. All he had to do was dial in Night Runner's PERLOBE ID. The satellite would find the Personal Locator Beacon signal, and a compass rose would show up on the heads-up display. An arrow would point right at Night Runner.

Greiner knew that all he had to do was turn a circle until the arrow pointed straight up in the display. Then keep looking until he locked onto the guy. The satellite could not lie. Sure, the gunny might be as sneaky as a fart in church, but he couldn't hide from electronic eyes and ears. Piece of jake, as Friel sometimes said.

Piece of jake? What the hell did that mean? he had wondered. He never had the nerve to ask that psychopath Friel. The gunny told him it was one of the hybrid expressions of the previous gunnery sergeant, Potts. *Jake* meant things were all right. Instead of *piece of cake,* it became *piece of all right.* He had to admit, there was a logic to it.

Greiner's fingers remembered the location of the right buttons to turn on the compass rose and GPS. He'd practiced in the dark. He'd practiced with noise and flashing lights going off to distract him. Riding in a moving tracked vehicle. With Friel slapping him on the back—all too cheerfully—to simulate the difficulty of concentrating in combat.

That Swayne. He knew how to train somebody. Greiner found the buttons. The lights came on. He cycled through the preprogrammed IDs and selected the gunny's.

He remembered Swayne's warning about leaving too many features turned on at once inside the goggles. Too much information could be worse than too little. True, the display was cluttered. Yet the arrow on the compass pointed out Night Runner's position.

Greiner turned his head. Couldn't be. He crouched behind his pile of stones so his movement couldn't be detected. All the while swiveling to his left.

Something must be wrong. *Damn!* After all that patting himself on the butt, he'd selected the wrong ID.

Somehow he must have hit the menu when Friel's ID came up. For he was staring at the hillock where Friel had hidden himself to the left. No, it was the right PER-LOBE number. Maybe a glitch in the power pack. He tapped on the dome at the back of his helmet. The arrow never wavered.

Greiner switched off the locator to clean up the display before his eyes. He inched up to the rocks, finding a new spot for his head to appear. Swayne might still be watching him. Or the gunny. They'd have his ass if he made the mistake of sticking his face out of a hole in the exact position where a sniper might have laid an aim.

He scanned the camp again. He should be looking at the man. But he saw nothing in the flat, open expanse of the desert. *Where the hell was the gunny?*

WHERE THE HELL was the chief? Friel wanted to know.

The gunny. Always playing games on him. Giving him the business for playing games himself. Sneaking around.

Creeping up on somebody. Disappearing right in front of your eyes. Big deal.

Okay, so the gunny was the best guy in the Marine Corps at playing Indian. Big surprise. He was an Indian. What else was he supposed to be, except good at creeping around, the son of a bitch?

But this wasn't the time for playing Sneaky-Pete. The sneakiest Force Recon Marine in the world should have given a signal by now. So the best shooter in the world could pinpoint him. Could cover his ass.

Friel thought about speaking out, just asking the gunny where he was hiding out. But no, the captain would have a cow. Friel figured he was already in the shit for trying to straighten out the FNG. The only guys the officers wanted talking on the radio were other officers.

Officers. He knew plenty of Force Recon Marines. Plenty of them were on teams run by noncoms. Plenty of guys got left alone to do their jobs and didn't have to have officers expecting them to run around like they had broomsticks up their asses. Maybe he ought to find himself another team, another detachment, hell, another company. Why stop there? Maybe he ought to get his ass out of this chickenshit outfit. Maybe he ought to put in for the SEALs.

He tried to see himself wearing that Navy Cracker Jack goofy suit. Nah, he wasn't so bad off he'd turn himself into a freaking squid.

Maybe the Army—

Friel's mind dug in its heels at the very thought. *The Army? Why not the Boy Scouts?*

Speaking of Boy Scouts, that's what the gunny was trying to make him into. The gunny—

Hey, maybe the chief wasn't playing games after all. Maybe he had fallen down and broke a leg or something. Friel had to laugh. Wouldn't that be funny? Sneaky Pete

himself with a busted leg. Laying out there too proud even
to make a radio call to get help.

Okay, maybe that wasn't too funny. He reached up,
fingered the buttons on his goggles, and turned on the
PERLOBE finder. He ran down the menu and picked up
the gunny's.

Figured. The piece of crap wasn't working. Instead of
pointing down to the camp, where Night Runner was supposed to be, the compass arrow pointed right up his own
ass, as if—

The screen in front of his eyes lit up in a starburst of
lights and colors, like a fireworks display.

His mind took a hike to la-la land. The damned goggles
had gone haywire?

He yanked them off his face.

No, the light show was still going off in his head. He
had been hit before. He knew the feeling. This was it.

He remembered the explosion at the helicopter landing
zone—what was it? Two missions ago? This was too
much like—

No, it wasn't. This was no explosion, except in his
head. No heat. No blast lifting him up and throwing him.
No hooks and needles ripping at his skin. Somebody had
hit him. His mind knew it, but his body could not do
anything. He should speak up now. But even as the
thought crossed his mind, a hand stripped the boom mike
away. Then his face was shoved into the hillock in front
of him, filling his mouth with sand and gravel. He felt his
arms being yanked behind him. He would have called out,
but he could not even breathe for choking on dust.

He tried to remember whether he had heard anything.
Had somebody snuck up on him without making a breath
of a sound?

He tried to remember if he heard something in his subconscious.

Nothing. He had not heard a thing. Had not felt even

a stirring of the air. He wondered if somebody had put a bayonet through the back of his neck. Because he had no feeling in his arms and legs. No feeling at all except for a need to breathe.

This was it. He had let down his guard. He had been so pissed off at his officer and his team that he had no longer been a part of the team. Or even a Force Recon Marine. He had just been one more crybaby. Now he was going to be be killed. If he hadn't been already.

The sparkling show inside his heads-up display began to dim. From out of nowhere, a fragment of a prayer he barely remembered flitted through his head: *Now and at the hour of our death, amen.*

Speaking in the voice of one of the Jesuits.

He couldn't remember the rest of the prayer. He was going to die without salvation. Ah, well . . .

Screw the Jesuits. Screw salvation too.

PRIVATE FIRST CLASS Simon Winston kept up his watch, glad that he could make a contribution to the Force Recon team of Captain Jack Swayne. All the way from the Operational Mission Command Center two hundred feet below the surface of Quantico, Virginia. Not since the mission in Montana had he been allowed to participate as much—the Marines liked to use Marines in even support positions like his own. Back then he had come up with the idea of using satellite surveillance of Swayne's team to guide them on tactical snowmobiles through a blinding blizzard. That had been his own invention; the Corps had adopted him because of its success. He had felt so proud that he had made that innovation. When Swayne had come into the tactical operations center, even before reporting to Colonel Zavello, he had looked Winston up. He had put a hand on his shoulder and thanked him for helping the team do its job. Never had Winston, whose job title was so secret that he couldn't even say its name, felt so proud. It was as if he had been given a standing ovation at a Yankees playoff game.

So the kid from the Bronx, who was assigned to real-time analysis of satellite surveillance, wasn't about to let down the Spartans now. He knew Captain Swayne would be counting on him, even if Swayne didn't even know he was in on this mission.

Winston's surveillance scope could be directed by a series of toggle switches like an advanced video game. The signals that he applied to the tiny joysticks, buttons, and toggles would be converted to electronic emissions directed upward to a relay satellite. A series of other relay satellites would carry the image around the curvature of the earth and direct the proper controls on the target satellite. In this case, KYMI-36, now above the Persian Gulf and scheduled to be on station for two more hours.

Winston used a standard pattern of surveillance of the target area. He would begin at the center of the target zone proper, the terrorist camp, and scan outward in ever-growing concentric rings as the satellite lens zoomed back.

The idea was, first, to confirm that there was a target where it was supposed to be. Second, that the size of the enemy force was as it had been projected. In a glance, he confirmed that the terrorists had not been reinforced and none of them had left the camp proper. So far, so good.

His second look covered the area within one mile of the zone. Swayne and his team had closed but had not attacked. He checked a digital counter at the top of his screen. A series of digital readouts told him the local time, Zulu time, with a countdown timer to each scheduled event. Taped to the side of his console was a list of the mission events. Already Winston had crossed off his earlier surveillance checks. He had made his reports, and nobody had paid much mind to them, because they were negative, which meant that nothing had changed from the intelligence summaries that had been forecast.

The checks within the one-mile circle assured everybody that the enemy had not sent out patrols that might interfere with Swayne's approach and the landing of the insertion helicopter. At irregular times he had watched the terrorists replace their sentries on outposts. During the evening, some of the outposts had been abandoned, as the terrorists joined the circle around the campfire to eat barbecue, drink American beer, and be merry terrorist-style. He would even read the labels on the beer cans.

Winston backed the surveillance lens of thermal images out to a five-mile range. Within that area, any intruders on foot could react to Swayne's attack and influence the action. At that pullback range, he could not identify individual thermal hits. But he could zoom in on each group individually and determine what they were. Round or oval dots would be a vertical thermal signature of a standing man. A linear thermal image could be a man lying down. But each time Winston checked one within the five-mile range, he found a deer or a coyote. Then, his heart thumped the inside of his chest as he recognized a round image about half a mile from the target zone, exactly at the landing zone. *If the terrorists—*

But once he zoomed in, he recognized that it was a hot spot in a hole. And after only ten seconds, the round image turned linear as a desert fox slipped into the night. Then a second. Then a third. The cluster of animals began milling in the night, until one thermal image mounted the other.

Winston smiled at first. Then his heart stopped. As a hand clamped onto his shoulder.

"The hell are you doing?"

"Colonel Zavello. I saw a hot spot on the LZ. I—"

"Hot spot my ass. Listen, kid, you want to watch animals screwing, wait to get off work and turn on the Discovery Channel."

"Sir, I—Yes, sir." What was the use? Besides, Zavello's grip on his shoulder was beginning to cut off his circulation.

Winston's fingers flew over the controls, and the satellite pulled back so he could resume his coverage. He had delayed his routine only a few seconds—actually less than the time that he had spent in trying to explain himself to Zavello.

The hand remained on his shoulder. He thought about trying to assure the boss that he would never jeopardize a mission, that he would never put Swayne's team in danger by a lapse in—

The hand came off his shoulder. It patted him on the head. Winston had never felt that Zavello even knew he existed, except as a target of his anger. The pat seemed to be telling him that everything was all right. He looked up to confirm it in Zavello's eye.

But the colonel had turned and stalked away, already finding another ass to gnaw on in the command center.

Winston kept a straight face. Inside, he beamed.

His eyes swept the countdown timer to the next event. Less than a minute before H-hour.

SWAYNE CHECKED HIS watch. Less than a minute before H-hour. Where the hell was the gunny? Why hadn't he—

"One, this is Two. Normandy is set."

Swayne felt a wash of relief. And surprise. Still. As many missions as he had been through with Night Runner, and the man could still astonish him. How could he have placed the contents of his backpack so quickly to strike the terrorists? Well, yes, he had had enough time for that. But also to do a thorough recon? And recover from the camp? And get into a firing position? In just the time it took for the three others to get forward?

Nothing less than amazing. Swayne felt lucky once again that Night Runner was on his side. And that the gunny was working at his own peak performance. The team needed that. It compensated for the drop in performance that a new guy would cost them. Besides, Friel had slipped a notch in Swayne's eyes too. For the past two missions, he had been so consumed with grief, hatred—whatever—that he had been more a worry than an asset to the team.

Swayne blamed himself. He should have forced him into shrink treatments. There was no stigma attached to it in Force Recon. Nothing more than routine sick call.

Because Force Recon Marines had to see so much gore, because they had to cause so much destruction, especially because they had to keep their mouths shut about what they saw and did, they were prone to mental and emotional stress. Far more than ordinary soldiers. Feelings of guilt had to be shut in. Feelings of shame were never allowed out. Yet the Marine Corps at least was smart enough to know that such feelings existed. So specialty shrinks had been contracted. Shrinks with no obligation to report anything back to Force Recon's chain of command. Unless the Marine was so damaged that he would be a liability to the team's combat performance, nobody would know what went on in those head sessions.

Swayne didn't need a shrink to tell him that Friel had fallen into an abyss of darkness, a rage he could not—or would not—suppress. It was wrong of him not to have sent the man into treatment.

Friel's verbal abuse of Greiner could have been foreseen. Hell, Swayne had known it had been just a matter of time until the kid from Boston snapped. Swayne had been in denial about it himself, thinking that this low-stress mission might be just the thing to oil the team and work out the mental kinks.

Thinking like that had a name. Denial. Swayne kicked himself in the head for that kind of delusional thinking. Maybe, he thought, he ought to see a shrink himself.

He hadn't heard anything in a while from Friel. That seemed unusual. He checked his watch. Ten seconds. Time enough.

"Spartans, report ready."

"Two is up. Three is at my side."

"FOUR IS UP," Greiner said. A chill ran through his body. The arrow on his PERLOBE finder had not been wrong after all. Somehow, Night Runner had done the work of two men in setting up the ambush and had returned from the target zone without being spotted. How could a man do that?

Greiner checked his digital clock in the heads-up display. Just as the visual alarm began to flash.

Strike time.

NIGHT RUNNER SAW the same alarm go off on his wrist, the brief flashing of his watch-dial light.

He put a finger to the button of his remote detonator, oblivious to the attack that would begin at his touch.

He was too busy right now to worry about killing a bunch of helpless, harmless terrorists.

ON SWEEP ELEVEN of the target zone for Team 2400, Winston picked up a huge hit. Just before the mission was to kick off, just at the edge of the five-mile ring was a cluster of thermal images. A formation of men approaching the camp?

The sudden pumping of adrenaline made his temples ache. His eyes blurred and he realized the meaning of the phrase "make your head swim."

He zeroed in with the toggle between his right thumb and forefinger, and zoomed up so fast his eyes began to dance again from the blur on the screen—the effect that analysts called Eye-vertigo, or I-vert. Too fast. And too

close. The lens took in only half-a-dozen linear images.
No sweat.

Winston could see they were animals. He pulled back.
A herd of animals to be exact. He remembered what he
had seen at the closeup. His mind told him. Goats. Sure
enough, once he had gotten the proper zone distance, he
could see a herd of about fifty animals. On each of the
rear flanks he saw the oval that would indicate the bird's-
eye view of the head and shoulders of two goatherds.

But where were the dogs?

There. Worrying the animals at the rear of the herd
were two smaller linear images darting back and forth.

Winston relaxed. A batch of goats and two peasants
were no threat to the mission. Unless—

He pulled his field of view back farther. He could see
Swayne's team splitting up as the H-hour digital numbers
flashed ever closer to zero.

He gauged the flock's direction of travel. They were
headed toward the camp. But on a line that would not
affect Swayne's mission. Judging from their rate of speed,
they would not be in the kill zone.

The worst-case scenario, the two men stumbling onto
an ambush and giving it away, would not happen. He
double-checked the clock. No, there wasn't time enough
for them to spring the trap early.

Then his mind went to work on why anybody would
be moving through the desert at night with a flock of
goats. The logical answer was to resupply the camp with
fresh meat. Meat so fresh it was still on the move, and
warm besides. Doing it at night would hide the fact that
there was a camp to supply.

But Winston, biting his lip, wasn't so sure. He knew
better than to let his mind provide benign reasons to explain potential enemy activity.

That was one mistake he would not make. So he began
typing, posting an update to the master situation screen. No

point in making a verbal alert. The mission was under way already, the attack imminent. Although there was a general air of quiet on the tactical communications net, and a hush in the tactical operations center, all over the room officers and analysts were whispering to each other. Zavello ran a tight ship. If anybody made too much noise during a combat mission, there had better be an emergency reason for it.

The thought made Winston reconsider. Was this an emergency? A herd of goats? *That's a neg, Simon,* he assured himself. *That's a big fat-butt negative.*

Any sighting of an enemy force would have required Winston to speak up.

But this was a herd of goats, for Uncle Pete's sake. To say something now would brand him an idiot.

So he began typing his report, his fingers clicking like cockroaches running through the silverware drawer. The low-level alert would appear on the master screens of the operations desk, the intelligence desk, and the command central screen in front of Zavello. A flashing icon would indicate the level of notification. A bright icon flashing quickly would command somebody's attention. Winston chose a dim-slow flash. He could add a tone with three levels of volume to increase the urgency.

He gave it no audio tone.

Then he went back to his screen. He searched the ten-to-twenty-mile zone outside the target area. To see if any mechanized forces were in range of reaction to the strike. Which was within seconds of kicking off.

He took a deep breath. He was glad there'd been no enemy to report. He wouldn't want anything to happen to those men on the ground. He wanted to check out their situation, but that would be a gaffe too serious to commit. Like the Secret Service detail surrounding the President, he was supposed to watch the crowd, survey the rooftops, scan the horizon, not gawk at the target of any enemy assassin.

Besides, he'd already been caught watching foxes fornicate. *Jeez, if that ever gets out . . .*

SWAYNE LOWERED HIS head so the first blasts could not wash out the images in his NVGs and ruin his night vision besides. He knew the drill well enough in his head. He and Night Runner had laid out the plan and briefed the rest of the team. They had rehearsed and refined it in Nevada. So although his head was down and eyes were closed to the flashes, he could see it as clearly as if it were a computer simulation running on the inside of his eyelids like a heads-up display.

The first explosion went off, a muffled blast, sending golden sparks in a fireworks display over the camp. This was the alarm clock, so called because it would awaken everybody in the strike zone. Night Runner had buried a small charge near the edge of the fire pit. The blast was loud enough to get the attention of a sleeping man, even if he was drunk. But not so loud that everybody would dive to the floor, as if the camp were under mortar attack.

Swayne counted down in his head. He heard sentries calling out to each other as they awakened. He heard calls from the center of the camp. The outposts yelled back to them.

Swayne did not understand their language, but by the tone, he realized what the guards were saying. They were telling men in the tents to go back to sleep. They were saying that somebody probably had left a beer can too close to the fire. They were assuring themselves and others that the camp was not under attack. Of course they would think that. There had been no follow-up explosions. No gunshots.

He visualized the scene in each barracks tent. Men might be leaning upon elbows. Might be sitting at the edge of their cots. Might be lying on the floor where they had dived, now getting up sheepishly because there was no attack.

In seconds, when they would be most vulnerable, getting to their feet, preparing to lie down, arranging blankets and pillows—

The det-cord went off. Three powerful explosions.

Swayne shook his head. Night Runner had done his job, all right. He had wrapped the cord around each tent, tucking the ropes of explosives—six times more powerful than the det-cord that had been developed for use in Vietnam—inside the sandbags. It was as if each barracks was the center of a shaped charge. The sandbags would direct the explosion inward. The concussion would kill a man, if the equipment, hung on the inside of tents and soon to be flying like shrapnel, did not.

Swayne waited for the large explosions. He had counted down past thirty seconds. Nothing. Five more seconds. Five more. Five more, and still nothing.

Swayne hadn't wanted to be any part of this killing exercise, had not wanted his team merely to be executioners. But he had not been given a choice. So the mission should be carried out with as much violence as possible. These terrorists should be—

NIGHT RUNNER TOUCHED off the main det-cord blasts.

He was not in the least concerned about the slaughter he had arranged down below. It bothered him a little that he had been late, that he had been preoccupied, that he would have the captain doubting him.

With the second touch of his remote detonator, the captain's worries would be eased. The bulk of the terrorist force would be killed in or near their beds. He would be getting far more out of this exercise for his team than simply killing a bunch of play terrorists.

Night Runner was more concerned about something

else. He aroused Friel from his stupor. The one he himself
had induced by a blow to the carotid artery in the sergeant's neck. Working fast, he had tied Friel's hands at
his sides and worked a length of pole he had picked up
at the camp through his elbows behind his back. Another
pole went behind Friel's knees, and a board was wedged
vertically between each pole the length of Friel's body.
This gave the kid from Boston a stiff back. Literally. Not
unlike Night Runner's own stiff and scabbed back. Good,
Night Runner thought, they would have a pain to share in
this, a replica of his own test of courage not a month ago.

The board made Friel easy to handle. Before he set off
the second set of explosions, Night Runner had propped
the man up on his knees and splashed water on his face
to awaken him. Now Friel, his knees spread apart, the
board forcing him to kneel erect, had to watch what was
going on.

Had to watch without speaking, for Night Runner had
taped his mouth shut. In a show of mercy, he had used
regular duct tape, and not the bad-ass duct tape that was
nearly impossible to remove without taking skin and hair.

Night Runner had stewed over Friel for months. Since
before the last mission in Kosovo. Friel had been traveling
down a one-way street toward out of control. Swayne had
held back, clearly waiting for his gunnery sergeant to take
the situation into hand. Night Runner, so decisive in combat, had resisted doing anything with Friel. Because he
did not believe any of the traditional methods of discipline
would have any effect. He had given the man many a
hard stare. He had spoken to him in private. Quietly. Perhaps too quietly. Friel was not the kind to take subtle
hints.

The captain had barked at Friel over the radio. After
the Kosovo mission, Swayne had disciplined Friel. Too
gently, to be sure, because his disobedience in the field
had saved their lives. Friel could not rest with that. Could

not accept that he was being given a break. He was a mean white kid from the mean streets of Boston. Always something to prove. Always resisting authority.

So. He had to be taught a lesson. It could not be a traditional Marine Corps lesson. Night Runner had to hit him where it hurt. Hit him where he lived. Make an impression that he would never forget.

Nothing could teach Friel how to behave in a team situation than to be removed from the team. Night Runner had thought about asking Swayne to leave Friel home. On second thought, that would not have done any good. The team would have been hurt by the loss of one of its integral parts. Friel would sulk, would stay drunk while the rest of the team was off on its mission. He would rejoin them later, nastier than ever. More sulky even than now. Nothing to be gained by that.

So Night Runner had decided to relieve Friel in the field. He'd decided to treat him like a shameful warrior, by shaming him, not in front of the rest of the team, but in his own eyes.

Disabled and made to watch the mission being carried out, Friel would have to realize that he was not as important as he thought. Swayne and Night Runner and the new kid, Greiner, could pull this off without Friel.

He knew Friel well enough. Watching without participating was his worst pain. He would never run to the captain to file charges. That would make him a snitch. He was a smart kid, and he would understand what had happened to him. After the camp was neutralized, Night Runner could come back to him and cut him loose. Friel could pick himself up and rejoin the team at the rally point. They would recover together to the pickup zone and leave Iran in their Stealth helicopter. Nobody would be expected to talk anyhow. That would give Friel enough time to reflect. By the time they got back onto a carrier in the Persian Gulf, Friel would get it. Or he would not.

Night Runner would not have to say a word. He would know by Friel's performance from then on whether the kid could be trusted in combat again. Could be trusted in garrison again, for that matter. How he acted toward his team—and especially Greiner—would tell Night Runner whether to ask Swayne to have him dismissed from Force Recon. Perhaps even from the Marine Corps.

Forget about psychologists. This was one warrior's way of dealing with another, misfit warrior.

FRIEL COULD NOT understand why he was still alive. Had he let the ragheads sneak up on him and bash him in the noggin? But why had they tied him up like a sacrifice at a convention of Satan worshipers? He could barely move. His fingers were numb from the tightness of ropes around his wrists and the pain of having something crimped between his elbows. He could move his eyes, but not his head. He could shift his weight, but only a little. And once, he nearly fell over on his face. So he leaned back, feeling the pain of the pole behind his knees, feeling lucky that he could still breathe, feeling confused that he was still alive, feeling exposed as the ambush took place in front of his eyes.

The remote ambush had been set up to his left on a hillside. Night Runner was to set it off—

There it was. Automatic devices began firing small-arms blanks from the hillside. One device simulated an automatic weapon.

The idea was to give the terrorists a target. After the explosions, the terrorists would remain frozen in their foxholes, in case they were under artillery attack only. They would not expose themselves. Unless they had a reason either to fight or run. The ambush kit was to give them that reason, make them think that artillery was not a problem, that a ground attack was under way.

Sure enough, several of the men in the outposts began

shooting. As he watched the edge of the field of view in his night-vision goggles, many more sentries simply left their foxholes to run away.

But they did not run far. Gunfire to his right. Grinder. Each time the man shot, one of the enemy dropped. Friel snickered. Four men down, but only two of them killed. Of the remaining two, one was writhing where he lay, and the other tried to low-crawl to safety. Friel could not help feeling superior. When he shot a man, the bastard—

But he wasn't shooting, was he? *Shit.*

Other men fell. Other men ran away. Two or three staggered from the wreckage of the tent frames and stumbled into the open, where they were shot down. One cluster of men fell all at once from a small explosion.

Friel recognized from the effect what gun had been used on them. His blowpipe. The 20mm missile launcher, with a high-explosive round set to proximity fuse. Like an artillery shell, it blew up before it reached the men, piercing some through with shrapnel, killing others with concussion.

But how? His head was still rattled by the blow he had taken. But he remembered damned well that nobody else on the team had carried the 20mm into this battle. Only he had such a weapon. It had been in his hands when—

How long ago was it? He couldn't say. But he knew damned well that he had been holding it not too long ago. Would one of the terrorists have taken it? No, a terrorist would not be using it on his own men.

Friel closed his eyes. *What the hell was going on?* Was this a daydream? No, the pain in his arms and legs as he knelt here crucified in the desert were all too real.

He opened his eyes. Below him, all movement had stopped. The attack was nearly over, and hardly any more shooting came from the positions where Night Runner, Swayne, and Grinder were supposed to be. Only the automatic ambush kit kept firing. Finally, that too began to peter out. Then all was silent.

He knew what was to happen next. He and Swayne were to move into secondary positions. Grinder and Night Runner would provide cover. On Swayne's word, Grinder and Night Runner would shift. They would observe the target zone for another minute or so. Then they were to pull back to a rally point, count noses, and slip off to a helicopter landing zone half a mile away.

A surge of fear coursed through him. He was going to be left here to die. The terrorists would find him tomorrow. Found and skinned. Boiled in goat fat. Eaten by ants. The bastids would—

No, Night Runner would never leave him. Neither would Swayne. They would count and come up one nose short back at the rally point. Night Runner would come for him. Night Runner would—

Night Runner.

He swallowed hard. No wonder he was still alive.

Night Runner!

The terrorists hadn't bagged him. The picture of his compass in the heads-up display flashed in his head. The arrow had been pointing behind him. He had thought he might have set the PERLOBE finder wrong. Or that the damned thing had been out of whack. But no—

Freakin' Night Runner!

The gunny had been giving him the stink-eye for weeks. Friel had been waiting for the chief to chew his ass. He had been planning to come back at him and drop the little item about saving the chief's ass in Kosovo. Night Runner hadn't said anything. As if he knew what Friel's comeback would be. As if—

Yes, only the Indian could have snuck up on him like that. That would explain where the blowpipe went. If the bad guys—

Night Runner had done this to him.

The chief, bug-eatin' bastid that he was, had beat him like a tom-tom.

Night Runner was trying to teach him a lesson.

Waves of emotion hit Friel. Relief that he was alive. Anger that the gunny had kept him out of this fight. Resentment that Grinder was in the battle, and he was not. Satisfaction that he would be given the chance to get even. *Night Runner, the bastid, low-life, dog-eating prairie scum.* He smiled. There would be a get-even time coming.

Even in his predicament, Friel knew that he was one up. The chief was still a Marine. A Force Recon Marine. No Force Recon Marine was going to leave one of his own in the desert.

Yes, he would come to get him. He would set him free. And one day—or night—Night Runner would have to turn his back on Friel. When he did—

Friel saw movement not fifty feet away. A pair of men had crept out of their foxholes and were low-crawling up the hill. Right at him. He could not read terrain as well as Swayne, but he could see a ridgeline as well as anybody. That ridgeline was keeping the two terrorists out of sight of the team.

All at once, Friel ran out of revenge. Just as he ran out of hypotheticals. He had been under attack before by superior numbers. So he had fought like hell. He had never felt as if the enemy would overcome him. He had developed a mental plan of action to deal with just that situation. He would keep on fighting. He would fight until an enemy was forced to kill him to save himself.

Surrender was no option in the Force Recon Marines. So Friel had already played out his worst-case scenario. Should he run out of ammunition and have no firepower to keep killing, he would fix bayonet and attack, attack, attack. Or else, he would evade the enemy and live to fight another day. If neither of those options were open to him, he knew what he would do. He would always have one blade—in his case, several blades stashed in his gear and on his body. Suicide was against everything the Jesuits taught. But he was not afraid of dying. Not even at his own hand. He would die on the battlefield and not in some interrogation room.

It wasn't that he was brave, but that he knew down deep in the core of himself, he was afraid. Afraid of spilling his guts under torture. Or because of the truth drugs. Forget that they had programmed his mind in the event of capture, in case such drugs would be used. He did not trust that kind of mumbo-jumbo. Nor did he trust himself.

Now he was faced with a situation far worse than even his worst-case. Two soldiers were coming right at him. The ridgeline ran directly to the hillock. They would pass to his side of the position. They would run right into him. They would find him trussed up like a roasted pig.

They would find him. If they wanted to, they could humiliate him. They could kill him. They could urinate on him. They could spit on him. They could drag him away. And there wasn't a damned thing to do about it. He couldn't fight. He couldn't call out. He couldn't run away like a coward. Dammit, he couldn't even kill himself.

Night Runner. Damn him.

NIGHT RUNNER KNEW he had to move fast. Or else the captain would catch him at his little game.

A wave of shame lapped at Night Runner. The idea of deceiving his captain didn't sit well. He should never have pulled a stunt such as this. Fine if Friel were an Indian. Or if Night Runner had cleared it with the captain first. He should have acted weeks ago, when Friel had first started hassling Greiner. He should have warned him openly. Then threatened him with military action. Then sterner forms of discipline. Finally, threatening with the worst, to bounce him out of Force Recon. Not this stupid little trick. This was fine for dealing with a Blackfeet warrior of a century ago. Not now. What the hell had he been thinking?

He scanned the horizon near Friel's position. His heart leapt. What he saw was only a blur, a brief flash of movement. But he recognized it. The head of a terrorist, wrapped in their distinctive check-pattern cloth. Moving up the ridgeline. Toward Friel.

"Something's up with Friel," he said over the mike. "I'm going to check on him." It was not a request. He wasn't leaving room for Swayne to call him back. He was on his feet and running, staying to the high ground. He knew it would expose him to the valley below, just one more stupid thing in a chain of stupid events he had set in motion. He had to stay high. Had to keep his feet. Had to catch at least one more glimpse of that head—*had to*.

WINSTON'S MIND FOCUSED on the combat routine. He had had to develop the technique over many missions with a Navy master chief standing at his shoulder whispering threats into his ear: *Keep your eyes moving. Don't spend too much time looking at things that might not be of interest. Don't spend too much time looking at things that might be too interesting. Remember, you're a Secret Service agent. You have to look for danger that the President cannot see. You're a Secret Service agent.*

Winston knew the problem all too well. Watching a screen—and even listening to radio traffic—could become all too mesmerizing. It was reality TV times ten.

The temptation was to look at the Force Recon team, to watch in wonder as they deployed. He had allowed himself to cheat on some of the missions in his early days on the job. But a few knuckles on the side of the head from the master chief and just one ass-chewing from Zavello had cured him of that.

He vowed to keep his eyes off the Force Recon team, to pay attention to what was going on around them.

He zoomed to a hundred-mile radius. The idea was to look for military response forces to come out of the populated areas and the scattered military bases. Most dangerous of all, to look for aircraft or airmobile forces to come from the only populated area large enough to sustain an airport, Mashhad.

Once the attack began, Winston kept his attention at long distance. The battle zone would be kept under the constant watch of operations and intelligence types. There would be enough sets of eyes on both the attacking force and the terrorists in the camp to identify threats and to give advice about how the Spartans could react to nearby danger.

Still, when the first report of a possible enemy force slapped his eardrums, Winston knew where to look for trouble. That damned herd of goats.

All at once, his sixth sense kicked him in the gut. Dammit, he had suppressed his intuitions after identifying the animals. He had followed the procedures to a T, but had ignored a hunch.

As he worked the toggle and dials, he cursed himself. He should not have been so quick to underestimate the enemy, so facile with an explanation why there'd be a herd moving at night. He should have reported the sighting with a higher priority.

His hands trembled as he focused the lens of his satellite onto the edge of the combat zone. He could see animals scattering. He zoomed in. Yes, they were goats. Maybe he hadn't let down Swayne's team after all.

He zoomed out.

"Crap!" he muttered in frustration as the controls acted sloppy, overshooting the resolution he wanted. The central body of the flock remained in place at the edge of the ambush. Thermal images organized a line behind the attacking force like soldiers.

The first idea that struck him was absurd. Swayne's

Force Recon team under attack by a herd of goats?

Utterly ridiculous. His mind wouldn't accept the notion, and to say it aloud would get him banished from the OMCC.

He fought the controls as his mind raced to review the situation. He had reported a low-priority sighting. His E-message had told the OMCC that he had seen a herd of goats approaching the ambush site. But now that he thought about it, he had seen only the linear images of perhaps half-a-dozen animals up close. He hadn't actually identified all the goats.

That recollection flashed on the retina of his memory. He had examined only a fraction of the herd in detail. He should have checked the animals goat by goat.

But he had been gun-shy. Because Zavello had caught him earlier looking at foxes mating, he'd dared not be caught looking at a goat screw too closely. He had shied away from the possibility of being ridiculed in the office. That personal fear had made him less of a professional analyst than he needed to be at a critical time. Now some Marine was going to have to pay for his mistake.

And what a mistake it was. He finished zooming and saw the reason the linear images had appeared as goats rather than men.

Decoys. The terrorists had traveled in clusters with the herd of goats, each man carrying what looked like an umbrella. Some kind of thermal umbrella.

The terrorists had made him look like an idiot, had fooled the most advanced satellite technology in the world with a damned parasol.

Winston felt a flush of shame at falling for a gimmick literally as old as the Trojan Horse, one that had been used on battlefields from Europe to Vietnam to Kosovo.

He couldn't help feeling a blush of admiration too.

But only for a second. The terrorists had busted his chops, using real goats and fake thermal goats to make him into a goat. Zavello was going to have his ass for brunch.

Winston would take his licks like a man. But he vowed he'd never leave the OMCC until he made up for his blunder.

FRIEL FOUGHT DOWN a scream. He had never been in a scrape like this before, had never expected to be left without options. Helpless to help himself. He wanted to scream. Tried to scream. The duct tape held it in. All he did was snort, like the crucified pig he was. He was going to die. He was going to die. He was—

No.

No, he would not die whining. With a huge effort, he tried to get a grip. There was one thing. Yes, it was lame, but there was one thing. If he could fall over on his face and play dead. No. Anybody who came upon him up here would recognize him at once as an intruder. They would run him through with a bayonet. Or stitch him up with a burst of automatic fire. And keep on running.

But if they mistook him as an Iranian caught off guard by their attackers, they might cut him loose. Or just keep beating feet, running away in panic. Ah, what the hell.

Friel pushed himself forward and stopped as a new concern hit him. What if he were to stick his face into the sand and smother? Then he realized, of course, that it would be one way to commit suicide and save himself from humiliation at the hands of his enemies.

Either way, he would die with Night Runner's name on his lips. He would take Night Runner's soul with him to hell, if he could. If he could not, he would bargain anything with the devil to get back here on earth and haunt the chief to his own end.

Next came the rage. He had lost feeling in his legs. Minutes ago, he had almost toppled by accident. Now he could not do it on purpose. The two terrorists were only ten meters away now, crawling. He could hear them gasping. They were going to run right into him unless—

One of them cried out. They saw him. Only one had a weapon. An AK-47. He pointed the automatic rifle in Friel's direction. The man's arms, trembling from the effort of crawling, could not hold the weapon up. Or was it something else?

The man lowered the muzzle and called out to him. Friel, giddy with fear, tried to curse at the terrorist. But not even that would come out right.

The man hollered at him. Now that Friel had not reacted, the terrorist was getting braver. He gestured with the AK-47. He shrieked. Friel recognized it. It was the challenge of a sentry, telling Friel to identify himself. Threatening to shoot. The man stood up, as if to show he meant business by making himself bigger.

Friel did not react. Because he could not. Except to widen his eyes as the muzzle of the AK-47 lifted to stare, one-eyed, into his face.

AS HE TOOK off running, Night Runner reset Friel's gun. He put the sight on visible laser, so he could shoot on the move just by watching the gun's beam on a target. He reset the arming switch off proximity, so the fuses in the projectiles would explode on impact. He had not covered half the hundred meters back to Friel's position when he saw the head come up. He could not believe his luck. Luck both bad and good. Bad because he was not close enough to completely see the situation, to see whether there might be another soldier behind the ridgeline. But good because the terrorist had exposed himself.

Night Runner planted his feet wide, coming to a halt in a standing firing position. Up came the blowpipe. A twinge of pain shot across his back, sharp and hot. Was that just one other mistake he had made? Testing his own courage so close to a mission like this?

No time to think of that. There stood the terrorist. As
soon as the head reflected the red laser beam, he squeezed
off one round. Then lowered his aim to the shoulder and
shot again. And again.

It was overkill, but Night Runner dared not take
chances. He had to finish the man and make any other
terrorists behind the ridge keep their heads down. Maybe
freeze or flee.

As he took off running again, Night Runner hoped that
somehow Friel hadn't worked himself loose, that he had
not gotten himself into the line of fire. Night Runner
would never forgive himself if he killed one of his own—

He could not, would not think of that.

Friel. He wanted to call out to him. But he dared not.

FRIEL SAW THE killing unfold. First the beam splashed the
terrorist's beard and flicked to his ear, then his shoulder.
For a second, Friel wondered if Night Runner was having
trouble deciding on an aiming point.

Then the man's head exploded, bursting, vanishing like
a vapor. The impact toppled the terrorist. A second round
hit him in the side and took off the left shoulder. A third
round cut the remainder of the corpse in half.

Friel was sprayed by a mist, and he knew by the thick
smell of it that it was the blood of his enemy.

The first thought in his head was that Night Runner had
wasted some shots. Still, he was glad of it. Because it
meant that the gunny was feeling some guilt. He might
even be afraid that Friel would get hurt and leave his own
ass in a sling. Friel felt a moment of satisfaction in that.

Not a long moment. For the second terrorist had picked
up the AK. Like the last one, this raghead was shouting
at Friel. He didn't need an interpreter to know that this
was not a plea to surrender. It was not an inquiry about
whether he was friend or foe. The terrorist was cursing
him out. He was bringing up the AK-47. He was going

to open up on Friel. No more questions asked. For all the bastard knew, it was Friel who had shot down his buddy, and not somebody in the distance. Not that it mattered. He was going to take out his revenge on Friel.

The man knelt and raised the rifle. Friel could not make out the full image. He knew the man was not exposing himself to Night Runner again. Friel felt as if he were being covered by a rifle bore the size of the Holland Tunnel. All of the night's darkness was focused at that one point. The point was aimed directly at him, a black hole. A punctuation mark, the bowling-ball-sized period that marked the end of his life.

Friel tried to remember some of his prayers. He could still have salvation. All he had to do was ask.

Screw it.

The tip of the AK-47 sparkled. Friel's eyes shut as he braced himself for the impact of bullets. He heard the crackling of rounds snapping past his right ear, then past his left.

He couldn't help laughing, although there was more hysteria than humor in his giggle. The stupid bastard had missed him. The crazy son of a bitch—

He heard shouts from behind him.

Then weapons opened up to his right and left.

For some reason, Friel was glad that he had not prayed. He did not want to be saved by God. He did not want to ask for salvation, because that would mean an acceptance of death. He wanted to be saved by the Force Recon Marines who had opened up on either side of him, their bullets and tracers ripping into the shadow of the terrorist in front of him, pulverizing him, throwing him backward downhill. Pounding him into the sand.

Until somebody shouted.

Friel didn't like what he had heard. That much shooting was not the kind of thing that Force Recon Marines would do. Not to kill just one man. And even if it had been

Force Recon Marines, they would not be using guns that made the sounds he had been hearing. They were not the sounds of weapons the team had carried on this mission.

The voice that had stopped the firing by shouting his order. It was not speaking English.

Friel hollered a curse word. A word muffled by the duct tape across his mouth. A word that was lost in the sparkle in his heads-up display just the instant before everything went black again.

ABBOUD BIN AZZAN and his band had closed to within half a mile of the camp where he had planned to spend the rest of the night and the following day resting when he heard the first explosions. No orders were required to his men, much experienced in fighting, day and night. They scattered into the desert, preparing to fight back in case of an ambush. When no enemy showed himself nearby, and more gunfire rose up ahead, Azzan called a huddle of his cell leaders. He listened to their advice.

All three of them recommended a change in plans. The first wanted to hold fast in the desert and not even send a man forward to find out whether the camp's officers were conducting night training, improbable as that sounded.

The second wanted to backtrack and lay up the night in a wadi.

The third wanted to detour and keep on pressing toward Mashhad, the holy city where they would find safety.

Azzan rejected all three alternatives. Had he listened to such timid advice, they would still be sitting back seaside, watching U.S. Naval ships come and go, planning a strike that would never happen. Instead, he had ordered the launch out, again against all advice. Because he had relied on his own instincts instead of their advice, a heroic deed had been done. A blow had been struck against the Great Satan, America.

So he said to them, "We go forward. I want to see what is happening."

Nobody protested. They knew he would not relent. Besides, each of them had lost a measure of honor to him because he had pressed for and been successful at the attack on the American ship. They had no standing to protest.

So they had gone forward on the run, to see for themselves the source of the firing.

Azzan wanted to know whether the camp would be as safe as he had thought. Surely, no American unit—nor even one of their flying missiles—would be wasted on such a trivial target. No fighters of note had come from that camp. No bands from there had even been in battle, except with their wives. Even their wives did not respect the men who would spend so much time at this camp and so much effort at avoiding the fighting against Israel and the other Satans of the Western world.

So it should have been an excellent hiding place. Azzan's two dozen men would easily share beds and food with the men there without drawing attention to themselves in the eyes of spy satellites. Before continuing their trek to Mashhad.

Even before Azzan reached a spot from which he could overlook the camp, he knew that it was under attack. The firing came from weapons not of their own issue. Besides it was not much of a fight. No shooting seemed to be coming from below. Instead, everything came from the high ground around the perimeter of the camp.

Using a pair of night-vision goggles bought at a high price from the French, Azzan studied the situation in one sweep of the glasses. Two tents were smoldering from small fires, and a third had collapsed on itself. He saw several bodies lying outside.

Devastation, yes, but light devastation. Neither bombs nor those flying missiles had been used. They would have left craters. Not the case here. Far to his left, he could see the sparkle of weapons firing. But he could see no men in the positions. That puzzled him, but he did not waste time puzzling for long. He continued to sweep the glasses across the landscape of the high ground.

Until right in front of his own position not thirty meters away, he saw a strange sight.

A man tied. Kneeling and tied, as if for torture. Or for execution. Below him on the hillside, two survivors of the attack creeping up out of the kill zone.

He ordered two of his cell leaders forward. The third would stay behind. He handed off the night-vision devices to the third cell leader. Then he joined the two groups moving toward the bizarre scene unfolding.

When one of the advancing terrorists was struck by explosive rounds and dismembered, he knelt too. He was just behind the figure that was trussed like a goat when the second man picked up the assault rifle and pointed it at the figure. Before Azzan could call out to stop the idiot from shooting, his own men opened fire. He saw the second man go down, and lost interest in the fight. He called for an end to the shooting, and his men obeyed him at once.

What drew his attention was this figure. Using a small penlight, he flashed it at the man's back. Even with the briefest glance at the pattern on the boot soles and camouflage of the trousers, he knew it was an American. On the ground beside him was a combat pack. Also American. The white skin behind the ear, the only place not covered with camouflage paint, confirmed it. Azzan could not believe his luck.

An American?

He could understand why they might be here. Perhaps bad intelligence had led them to believe this was an important target. And had they waited half an hour, it would have been. Azzan and his band might have been preparing a meal. Or conducting a strategy meeting. Or they might have been in prayer. Or just getting ready to sleep. They would have been caught in the killing zone.

He could not divine why the American was tied up like this. Perhaps the pair had captured him. Perhaps they had gone down to join the fight. It did not seem possible men as brave as that could exist in a place like this. Or as stupid. They would leave such a prize as an American special-operations soldier unguarded?

He would not make such a foolish mistake himself. Already he knew that another American had attacked from their right flank. Probably more. At the minimum, such teams operated in groups of four. Most of them eight. Some sixteen or more.

He could deploy his men and fight. Perhaps they might win, for his own men were as highly trained as any American unit. Although they might not have the same quality of high-technology weapons.

Azzan didn't need to kill any of the American intruders to gain glory for his cause, though. He knew that all he would have to do was take this one with him to Mashhad. Just one American could have many, many uses.

He knew how to multiply his forces. Simply keeping a security force in place would gain him time. That force would not even have to fight to the death. All they would have to do was keep pulling back along their route to the holy city. Such a tactic could delay a force five times the size of Azzan's.

Enough analysis. He stepped forward and swung the butt of his AK-47 into the face of the American, catching him on the chin, a blow powerful enough to topple him over backward. Azzan pulled a dagger and cut the ropes at the knees.

A few quick instructions to his cell leaders set everybody in motion. One cell would set up the first delay maneuver. A second would find an alternate position from which to defend. The first cell would overlap the second. And so on, all the way to the holy city.

The third cell was to take turns with the American. Two men at a time would grab on to the ends of the poles behind the man's back and they would drag him until he awakened. Then they would escort him under his own power.

Azzan would hang back and direct his men in the delay. He did not trust anybody else to do as well as he could. Besides, he wanted to prove something. The Americans and the Jews never gave his fighters credit as military technicians. They tried to paint them merely as fanatics who would strap bombs to their bodies and cars and kill themselves for their cause.

He would enjoy teaching these Americans a lesson in military tactics on his own ground, the desert. Ground that he knew and understood better than anybody. He had trained his fighters. They could outfight anybody. Special forces. Army Rangers. SAS. Israeli commandos. He had fought them all. He had suffered casualties, of course. In war, that was to be expected. But he had bloodied them all as well, and wiped out more than one group of invaders. Neither the Americans nor the Israelis ever complained about those losses. Only the children and civilians injured in shootings and bombings. Trying to create their own martyrs while mocking the martyrs of Islam. Too sheepish to admit their soldiers had been defeated in battle.

No, there would be no indignation over the losses of intruders.

No martyrs in the desert, only bones of men who died anonymously, men whose families would be told they had perished in training accidents, their bodies burned beyond recognition. Partly cremated bodies buried. Cremated remains of the homeless found dead in cities across America.

The thought brought a crooked smile to Azzan's crooked face.

NIGHT RUNNER, LIVING up to his name, had reached full stride, skimming across the sand like a lizard on a hot day. His heart leapt at the sharp report of an AK-47 on automatic. His first instinct was to hit the ground, but he realized at once that the gunfire was not aimed at him.

That was no comfort. He felt worse that the shots might be intended for Friel. He had tied Friel up like a sacrificial lamb and left him to die without knowing—

An array of weapons opened up in response to the AK-47, and this time, Night Runner dived and rolled, reacting by instinct. Even as he realized once again the gunfire was not for him.

Again, he did not feel any comfort in that. Only confusion. Who was doing the shooting?

He crept forward on his hands and knees, moving as fast as he could toward the ridgeline. What kind of enemy force had escaped the powers of detection in his senses? He had spent time in Friel's position. He'd had no hint that so many guns could be close enough to overrun the spot so quickly from below. Had he lost his powers to recon?

No, he admonished himself. There had not been a force big enough to come out of the terrorist camp with that amount of firepower. If they had, they would have given themselves away shooting at the ambush kit.

Whoever it was had come from the desert. A patrol? He did not know. He could not say. Somehow, he had suffered a lapse in his senses. He needed to get to the top of the ridgeline so he could see how.

"Night Runner, this is One."

Damn. Swayne. How was he going to explain to the captain the stunt that he had pulled? The stunt that made any of Friel's screwups pale in comparison.

• • •

SWAYNE WAS PISSED. Things were happening that his mission briefing and battlefield intuition had not made allowances for. He had not heard from Friel for far too long. Friel always had a comment. Swayne had to chew him out on every mission for shooting off his mouth with his acrid Boston-Irish accent. Swayne had come to expect at least a comment over the air, and had come to depend on it almost as a form of Friel reporting his status. Nothing this time, though. Something definitely was wrong.

And the gunfire. Where the hell had that come from? Friel being quiet was one thing. Being quiet when the enemy was at hand was too far-fetched for Swayne to grasp. He slid back away from his position and found the spot where Night Runner was to have set up a secondary position. Night Runner had been there and left. He could see footprints. Although Swayne was no tracker, he could tell that the set of tracks leaving the spot were spaced too far and too deep to be sneaking around. The gunny had been running at top speed.

Swayne pulled back farther, calling for Night Runner to report. He had to have information. He had to have tidbits for a plan. And quickly, to adapt to the new situation of an enemy force moving into the area. Probably from outside the terrorist camp. Maybe there had been a security patrol—no, the laxity inside the camp made that unlikely.

It had to be that a second force had moved into the area and reacted to the Spartans' attack.

Now he had not heard a word from anybody on his team. How could so much go wrong with such a simple mission?

"Spartans, this is One, report."

"Two, on the move toward the gunfire."

A pause. Friel should be putting in his two cents worth

by now. He did not. Nothing but silence until Greiner spoke up.

"This is Four. Holding in my alternate position."

Swayne's mind dealt with the new situation. Night Runner on the move meant that he would soon have some tactical information that would allow Swayne to outline a new plan. Meanwhile, he decided to gather up Greiner and begin moving to back up Night Runner.

"Spartan One, this is Eagle One."

Zavello. The one-eyed colonel had tuned in, of course. With all the other Force Recon teams deployed tonight, Zavello would have to be keeping an eye on this one. Maybe he had not heard Friel spouting off. Maybe he would not read the post-mission transcript. Maybe—

"Spartan One, respond."

Yeah, and maybe the colonel was calling to take his pizza order for when they landed back on American soil.

"This is Spartan One." *Cue the ass-chewing*.

"We owe you an apology up here," Zavello growled. "We had our IR satellite monitors focused elsewhere. We had no coverage around your area. Somebody up here was counting bodies instead of providing security for you. Now we have spotted the force that moved right into your rear area from the west."

Swayne bit his lip. He didn't need the apology now. No amount of regret was going to undo the situation. What he needed was intel. "How many, what type, what vehicles, what direction, location of Spartan Three?"

"Two dozen. On foot. Moving northwest. In separate squads."

Swayne detected a hitch in Zavello's voice. He already knew that he was about to hear the worst before it came.

"Spartan Three's PERLOBE indicates that he was over-run. His beacon is moving northwest with one element of the enemy force."

"Damn." Swayne didn't care that he had transmitted the

word. He was too disturbed that Friel had not sounded
the alarm, had not made his own report. That could mean
only one thing. That the PERLOBE that was being taken
away from the ambush site was pinned to the body of a
dead man. Or else, the dead man had been left behind and
the PERLOBE was being hauled off with the rest of
Friel's equipment.

The tactical officer in his head spoke up to suppress his
emotions. "Give me the disposition of the force. Are all
the bandits moving away?"

"Negative. The force is dispersing. One element of
eight bandits remaining on site. A second element working into position maybe a hundred meters to the northwest. The third element moving out with Spartan Three
at a good pace."

The picture formed inside Swayne's head as soon as
Zavello described it. A tactical maneuver that he would
have expected from a conventional Western force. He
knew at once that he was up against some people with
military smarts. Definitely not like those who had given
their lives in the valley below. He factored in the new
data and began working out some way for his three men
to take on a force eight times larger. It never occurred to
him that he should not. He only needed to work out how
he would.

NIGHT RUNNER HAD heard the exchange between Zavello
and the captain. Now, as he lay below the crest of the
hill, he did not have to raise his head to see what was
going on. Like Swayne, he could paint a vivid image in
his mind. Like Swayne, he could weigh the alternatives.
Trouble was, he had a much greater urgency than Swayne.
Night Runner had put Friel at risk to lose his life.

From deep inside his chest came the shriek of a warrior.
He fought to suppress it. The warrior wanted to charge.
Some braves of his tribe had made reckless charges in the

past. Most of them had died. With honor, to be sure, but their lives wasted. Certainly, he might not have to live with his blunder if he were to attack the force in front of him. That might get him out of his fix here on earth. But how would he reconcile himself in the afterlife? When his soul met that of Friel's, how could he even bear to ask forgiveness?

No, he had been reckless enough already. He could not—would not—compound one boner with another. He had things to do. To be able to go after Friel with honor and to fight with a clear head later.

Above all, he had to make sure that nobody else was going to get hurt on his account. He backed away from the ridgeline and ran toward the spot where Greiner and the captain might expose themselves to the enemy force now in position to ambush them.

He might not be able to do anything for Friel. That didn't mean anybody else would have to be hurt because of his stupidity.

ALL GREINER'S NERVE endings had come alive. They felt like downed electrical wires sizzling on the ground. Of course, he had known there would be fighting. He had expected it. Even looked forward to it. But the fighting would be against an enemy he could see. Just as it had been moments ago, when he had taken several of the terrorists out with carefully aimed shots. Sure, Friel would bitch him out for wounding two of them instead of killing them instantly. But he had done his job. He had created casualties. He had not let anybody approach their positions. Or had he? Was it his fault that Friel had been taken?

No. It couldn't be. Could it?

A Force Recon Marine captured? He had never heard of that. Was it because nobody ever talked about it? Or because it had never been done before? And how could it have been done? Especially Friel? Especially without the man uttering a single word, when he had a word for anything? Everything. All the time.

It startled Greiner when the blur of the captain flew into the field of vision in the goggles. He had to fight back the urge to throw down on his own man. He had heard about that in the rehashing of the team's last mission. The guy that he had replaced had actually opened up on Night Runner.

Now that he had been in the man's shoes, literally, he could understand. It was a snap reaction. But he caught himself.

"Come on, Greiner." The captain shot past him. Greiner got to his feet, turned around once, and began running. Tentatively at first, because it always took him a few strides to get used to moving at top speed in his NVGs.

The captain reminded him by his example to keep to a tactical status. Swayne's submachine gun swept to the front and to the right. Greiner reminded himself to cover the left. Every fifty feet or so he pulled up and turned a circle, stopping to check to the rear to see that nobody followed. Then he dashed forward to close on the captain.

Just as Greiner was about to draw abreast, Swayne dove to his right. Nobody had to tell Greiner what to do. He might be the new guy, but they had trained him well. He had dived in practice onto hard ground, onto piles of rocks, onto asphalt, and once even into a bed of cactus— the CUTE landing, Friel called it. Greiner couldn't figure out the acronym. The letters didn't make sense. Just one more thing not to like about Friel. One more thing among—

Greiner hit the ground almost the same time as the captain, without knowing why he had been given his cue to do so. He rolled, adjusted his goggles, and focused in the direction Swayne was pointing his rifle. He swiveled his feet, looking for the target.

There!

A wave of the hand. Night Runner? A second later, the speaker in his ear crackled to confirm.

"Hold what you have. This is Two, coming in." Greiner shifted his position once again so he would not be pointing his rifle where Night Runner would come over the high ground. He was already intent on covering the left flank and the rear, his areas of responsibility. He stole a glance over his right shoulder and saw the gunny slinking toward Swayne's position. He recognized a hand signal of two fingers cutting like a pair of scissors. They were going to shut off their mikes. No concern of his. He turned a quarter turn to the left, to watch their six.

He was going to do his job, no matter what. He was going to stay with this team at all costs. He was going to help them recover Friel. Not that he was all that crazy about Friel. That would be their mission now. He was sure of it.

Greiner felt a swelling in his chest. He knew what it was. He was proud of himself. He was going to make it as a Force Recon Marine. Never would he be allowed to tell anybody outside his unit. He didn't need to. It was enough to know he'd proved he belonged.

AZZAN HAD MOVED up within the circles of the conventional military, not just by his political and family connections. Yes, he was a Saudi prince. Yes, his father had been the top general in the Saudi Arabian Air Force. That was his ticket into the country's top military schools. His admission to the schools of the United States Army too.

He had attended the U.S. Army's armor officer advanced course at Fort Knox. An elementary military education, something he could have picked up just by reading. Not necessarily classified documents, either. The armor tactics of General Patton, Field Marshal Rommel, and the Israelis in the Yom Kippur war had not advanced so much over the years. At least not in the training that was being given to U.S. Army captains and majors and the handful of allied military officers that were allowed into the schools.

Two years later, he had attended the Command and General Staff College at Fort Leavenworth, Kansas. There the Army trained staff officers at a much higher level. What Azzan had studied was not so much the tactics and strategy courses being offered there. No, he had been more interested in the mind of the American military officer. Americans, like any other military force, considered themselves the superiors of their enemies and allies alike. For instance, the U.S. Army thought certain it could meet the Soviet Army in huge numbers and defeat it. In fact, it had founded defensive strategies on math formulas. Just crunch the numbers and whip the Red Army in Europe.

Azzan had to laugh at that.

He had predicted in his global political thesis that there would never be a European battlefield like the world had seen in its two previous global wars. He had theorized that the Soviet system would crumble. He had chided the American military, including the Command and General Staff College faculty, about fighting the last war. Terror was the weapon of the future. He wrote it. Since then, he'd proven it.

The Army major for grading his paper had been gentle. In an arrogant way. He had ridiculed Azzan's thesis. Even so, Azzan had received a 97. That was because the word had traveled around the school that he was a spoiled Saudi prince.

Azzan had had to laugh about that. They had dismissed his concepts, which had since become true with the fall of the Berlin Wall and the dismantling of the Soviet system. Yet they had given him the highest grade because they did not want to offend him.

Mostly, they did not want to offend his father, who controlled thirty-four percent of active Arab oil fields.

Azzan had been right. His predictions about the Soviet Union had been accurate. Azzan had personally used much of his wealth to realize his prophecy of terrorism as the ultimate modern weapon against capitalist states.

During the course of his career, he had used what he had learned about the mind of the American officer as his primary weapon. What he knew about United States arrogance was more lethal than his ability to plant explosives. Or to train killers willing to give their own lives to take out an enemy.

Azzan understood infrared surveillance techniques. He knew the capability of American satellites to cover the world, except for a few periods of the day.

None of the United States military schools had let him have access to classified information. No, he had had to sop up that information over drinks at the officers club. As long as he bought, the Americans had talked.

But even that was slim help for what he needed to know. The kind of details he needed, including file videos of actual imagery, he'd had to buy. Money had never been a problem. He had always had access to secrets that most military officers in the United States never even got to see. They did not have the need to know. Whereas, on his road to becoming one of the world's chief terrorists against the West, he did have a most urgent need to know.

That's why he knew to travel at night. Not even darkness could hide him from the eyes of those spy satellites overhead.

Buying a herd of goats was nothing to Azzan. It was even a practical thing to do, because keeping the animals meant there was always fresh meat in abundance. That made his men happy. It also meant that their thermal images could be disguised. Not entirely, of course. It cost him a little more money to do that.

He had invented the device itself. An umbrella was the

basic structure. He had hired a French technician to over-
lay the umbrella with a netting in the shape and size of a
goat as seen from above. The whole thing had been wired
with fabric able to conduct electricity. All of this was
wired to an ordinary set of flashlight batteries that added
three pounds to a man's combat supply kit. By day, his
troops could travel with the umbrellas folded, if they traveled at all, which was not a good idea after the strike on
the Navy ship. More often, they simply holed up under
cover. The umbrella, which was camouflaged in desert
tones, could be employed both as a sun shade and a blind.

Azzan's idea was to move at night to a desert camp of
amateur fighters. They would accept him because of his
reputation alone. They would be only too happy to rub
elbows with somebody who had actually struck at the in-
fidels.

That he would be bringing a supply of meat to them
would clinch the deal. They would do exactly as he ordered, feasting and remaining in view of American spy
satellites until the pressure eased.

The would-be terrorists would ask for training eventually, if not for money for new arms and equipment. Azzan
would grant them some of both. But not enough so Western analysts would consider the camp a threat.

Now this. Against all odds, this camp of play freedom
fighters was under attack.

Azzan put his mind to work on what might ensue. He
had an American in custody. An enemy this deep into Iran
would be a precious asset to the Americans, a deep-strike
special-operations team, perhaps a group from Delta
Force. Or Force Recon Marines.

Now that the shooting had begun, the Americans would
have to be pulled out of the fight. They had done their
damage. Possibly, they had taken video pictures to document the killing of innocents. Yes, fighters as poorly

trained and ineffective as these peasants were innocent.

But how would they extract themselves?

Helicopters. A no-brainer, as the Americans would put it. A target this easy would be expected to have been destroyed. The Americans would expect to meet their escape craft nearby and fly to safety even before the Iranians could respond.

Now the equation had spun out of balance. He had captured an American. He could not explain it to himself, could not even imagine how a fighter of this caliber would be tied up at the edge of an ambush zone. It would not have been done by anybody inside the camp. And he had seen no evidence of anybody outside the camp.

It did not matter. Azzan put the problem to the back of his mind.

What was important was getting the American to Mashhad, where Azzan could decide how best to use him to advantage.

As long as he had the American under his control, he could dictate the battle.

He knew these special-operations types. He had studied their minds more closely than any others. Conventional officers had not concerned him at the United States military schools because he would seldom have to face them, except when he was attacking them on his own terms. But the special-operations types, now they were a breed that interested him. They were well trained in his kind of battle. They were the ultimate warriors, an enemy he could admire. They could endure pain. They had access to high-tech weapons. They would be troublesome in a fight, difficult to pin down. Conventional forces would establish enormous bases. They would become targets just by their habits and their existence. The special-operation troops were another matter. They could live free of such comforts as tents and cots and prepared meals and all the dedicated supply lines needed by the bases.

The special operations units needed no such anchors to drag around behind them. They could dig holes in the open and establish blinds in the desert. Stay under camouflage by day and travel—and strike—by night. They could live off the land, distill their own water, direct air strikes, and lash out with exotic weapons, inflicting damage and casualties. They were a worthy enemy. He respected them.

They still had that central weakness. That sense of arrogance. They could not get out of their own skins. At the base of everything, they were Americans. Arrogant. Creatures of habits. Raised in comfort. Tied to obsolete mind-sets like decency and loyalty, to human concepts like friendship.

Because of these things, even against orders from higher headquarters, if necessary, they would be coming after this American soldier that he had in his possession.

Of that he was certain.

So Azzan put his head to work on the next step in his enemy's logic. This unit, whether the larger Delta Force or a smaller team of Force Recon Marines, would have a helicopter nearby. The helicopter would be their first choice of a crutch. They would use it to try to recover their man.

They had other high-tech weapons and devices. He did not fear these things. Because he knew about them. He had paid good money, in francs, to a member of the French government's intelligence service. He understood the new technology. That understanding and his knowledge of American arrogance would give him what he needed to defeat these Americans with their own devices.

They did not understand the mind of their enemy. They were quite incapable of knowing how far a man with a just cause could go, the sacrifices he would be willing to make.

For the love of Allah, they did not even know their own minds. Just one more point to his advantage.

Azzan called a council of his cell leaders. With a smile playing at his lips, he told them what measures to take, what sacrifices to make. They listened. They nodded. Nobody dared question him. They had seen him take questions before, on the previous operation that resulted in the bombing of the United States ship. Somebody had disagreed with his timetable. Azzan had reached across the conference blankets where his leaders had been assembled. He had grasped the man by the hair and pulled him forward. Then, in an opposing motion, he had slid the blade of his dagger across the dissenter's throat.

Over the gush of air, the gurgling and gasping, Azzan had asked if there were any further questions. There were none.

There were none now.

SWAYNE SHOOK HIS head. Had he actually heard what Night Runner had told him? He studied the face of Robert Night Runner, gunnery sergeant, U.S. Marine Corps. Could this really be a Marine? Or was this a Native American in the most primal sense? How could the man have laid such a primitive punishment on Friel? While they were under fire? Was Night Runner pulling his chain?

Night Runner must have seen the look in his face. "I'm not kidding, Captain."

Swayne shook his head. No, of course not. That was no possibility. Not out here. The man would never joke around in a combat situation.

He would most certainly not lie about what he had done. Nobody would have the nerve to tell his commanding officer that he had pulled such a stunt unless he had actually done it and the stunt had gone wrong.

A part of Swayne's brain kept poking at him from his

subconscious. Was it trying to tell him that this was not
the time to be evaluating—doubting really—his subordinate's leadership? Yes, Friel seemed to have gone over
the edge. Swayne had known that he would have had to
deal with the situation once they were back from the field.

Night Runner had already dealt with it. In the most
bizarre way. Now Swayne was going have to deal with it
too.

First, there was the problem of getting Friel back. If
they could just do that, Swayne could handle the issue as
a case of bad judgment.

He tried to give voice to his next thought: "If we can't
get him back—"

He could not complete the sentence. It was hard enough
to think it. But speak it, never.

Swayne put that thought out of his head and let his
mind go on automatic. One part of him considered all the
resources at hand. Another part began putting those resources to use. How to get Friel back? Recover the mav-
erick sergeant and the rest of the problem goes away, he
told himself. Knowing all the while it was not true.

The first problem, of course, was to get permission to
do it. Swayne made the briefest of SITREPs to Zavello.
Leaving out Night Runner's story.

The colonel already had a grasp of the situation, what
with the PERLOBE signal and the reconnaissance satellites overhead.

Bullshit on the spy satellites, thought Swayne. How
come nobody had told them of the approach of the enemy
force? How could anybody overlook a platoon of terrorists moving up on their rear flank?

No, Swayne told himself. Forget whining and deal with
the situation at hand. Worry about the mistakes that had
been made once they had landed back in the world. Take up
the matter in a debriefing.

Clearly, the terrorists knew what they had in their hands. They had deployed quickly to protect their captive. That was a good sign. It meant that Friel was alive. These terrorists, whoever they were, would not go through so much trouble to deploy and run if they did not have a live American in their possession.

Swayne made his radio calls, first to Zavello to give a report and request a change in mission, second to bring in Greiner for a face-to-face. Even as he told the kid what they'd be doing, he held his breath and waited for a reply from halfway around the globe.

When Zavello's voice crackled in his ear, Swayne's heart leapt, unsure of whether he was under attack by terrorists or the one-eyed colonel.

"Spartan One, this is Eagle One," Zavello growled. "Permission granted for mission add-on, as briefed."

"Spartan One, wilco." Swayne's tone communicated his thanks.

Zavello broke radio protocol to communicate his own emotion. "Get Friel back, Captain. Bring that kid back home."

The *or else* did not need to be spoken. It was right there in the tone.

EVENT SCENARIO 19

SWAYNE GATHERED HIS team close enough to murmur with microphones off. Night Runner and Greiner. The group seemed so small, so compact, and so quiet without Friel.

They understood the overall concept he'd briefed on the air to Zavello, Swayne's plan to recover Friel. Now he gave them the details of how they'd get to the LZ. Once there, he'd tell them the rest. Maybe by then, Swayne thought, he'd have figured out the rest.

The Spartans pulled back away from the hill. Not much point in engaging the delaying force. It was exactly what the terrorists wanted. Thus, it was the last thing that Swayne was willing to do.

As they maneuvered away from the ridgeline and clear of direct fire, Swayne's team began running at a tactical double time. Two men always on the run, overlapping a third man, who kept his weapon pointed to the rear. They could move fast this way. Two men would set up and wait for the third to catch up. Then one of the two would stay in place, while the other joined the rear security man to move ahead. It gave the Marines a chance to catch their breaths and to put distance between themselves and terrorists.

Distance meant time to think. Swayne thought he could gain even more time once they reached the helicopter LZ.

ZAVELLO ORDERED WINSTON—with a soft growl and a hard scowl that would have peeled the paint off an armored personnel carrier—to keep his electronic eyes on the terrorist unit.

"And don't go to sleep." Zavello scowled at him, and Winston knew what he meant. *Again.* The accusation was all too plain.

Shame prickled Winston's skin. But not for long. Because the terrorist unit that had been in a delay position began to move. Not as Swayne had predicted, though. Instead of moving away from Swayne's position, leapfrogging as it had been doing, it reversed direction.

"Spartan, this is Eagle Four-Five Bravo. One element, seven men, has begun moving in your direction."

SWAYNE, NOW LYING in position as rear security for the other two, nodded his head. "Roger." It was one of the possibilities that he had considered but had not expected. Once the terrorists realized that he was not going to beat his brains out against an entrenched force, they would very likely move. Either to join their comrades, or to come after him.

He realized that a truly good unit would come after him. To keep up the pressure. To maintain contact. Like the gazelle that would follow a pride of lions on the African savanna at a safe distance, the terrorists, if they were any good, would want to keep track of their enemy. Unlike the gazelle, they could also do some damage. For instance, by taking the LZ under fire when the Marines tried to board their aircraft.

Swayne had halfway hoped that this was not going to be a good unit. Things would have been so much easier. If they would only drop their guard. If they would let him break contact and get to the helicopter. But he would never allow himself to let such a hope cloud his judgment about what an enemy might do. He had the cardinal rule to obey: *Never let an enemy's capability be judged in the light of your own wishful thinking.* That one solid tenet of thinking had kept him out of trouble on past missions. He would never fall victim to such a thing, no matter how bleak a situation looked. This situation, for example.

Okay, so the terrorists had presented him with new circumstances to consider. They were things he had already sifted through his gray matter. If his team could keep out of range of direct-fire weapons, the Spartans could continue moving at top speed using the leapfrog technique. They could meet the helicopter and lift off, leaving the terrorists isolated.

On the other hand, if the terrorists closed quickly enough, it might be too dangerous to let them start shooting, even blindly. He remembered one other attack on a helicopter in a landing zone. As the team was trying to extract from a strike like tonight's, in fact. That had turned into a disaster, including the loss of Gunny Potts.

Swayne would err on the side of caution. He threw out a pair of concussion grenades, after setting them to remote detonation. A new feature had been added after the last mission in Kosovo. Each man's grenades could be operated on a discrete frequency, so one Marine would not set off another man's grenades, perhaps even as he was arming them. Yet Swayne could select the frequencies of his men and detonate grenades when he knew it was safe to.

"Hold what you have," he ordered over his radio mike.

"Roger," Night Runner said, "Two and Four have you in sight."

"Boomers out. Remote fuse." Swayne began running toward his men. By the scenario that he had given them, there was no need to explain any more about what was to happen. They were going to ambush the terrorist force following them toward the LZ. Seven men would have little chance against the weapons—and the boomers—of the Force Recon patrol. That was the plan, and simple enough. Hit them hard, then get to the helicopter.

WINSTON STUDIED THE Spartans' tactics as he saw them unfold. It was clear that one group of terrorists was going to be stung. That gave him a moment to feel relieved. If the team could get out of this, if they could recover Friel, Zavello might not blame him for—

No, he could not allow himself to begin daydreaming. He had a job to do. That job was not watching reality TV unfold. Watch the crowd, he reminded himself. He shifted the focus of the satellite lens back to the position where the other of the two elements of the terrorist force had—

Three elements. There were three elements now. One of the bands of terrorists, the one with Friel's PERLOBE, had split off from the others.

Now the second band was dividing as well.

Winston did not dare sit on something so hot. He alerted Zavello.

Zavello studied the screen for a moment. He had seen events unfold because he had never really taken his eyes off the group of terrorists with Friel's beacon. They had to have that Marine back. It simply would cost the United States too much if the Iranian government kept him.

This Administration had entered its lame-duck period. People trying to build a legacy. They needed something big, a legacy in the history books as big as Moses parting the Red Sea, something, *anything* that might undo all the scandals. As if that would happen.

But that did not matter to Zavello right now. No scandal had the potential of doing so much damage to the reputation of special operations as this one did. This could rank right up there with the Disaster in the Desert, as it was called after the failed attempt to rescue hostages at the American Embassy in Tehran. Now they were back in Iran again. And another disaster would not do. Heads would roll.

Zavello didn't care if his own head was on the chopping block. What concerned him was the information that this Marine might have about this operation and previous operations. Friel was not a man with strategic value. But he had tactical information about United States participation in Kosovo. In Iraq. In Africa. In South America. Hell, *in Canada,* if you wanted to dredge up an international incident that had been scarcely avoided a couple years ago.

Those were only the missions that came to mind in which Friel had played a part. No doubt, Friel would know of other operations. Friel knew facts that the enemy would be able to get out of him, which could be persuasive enough for the rest of the world to understand that the United States had been involved in missions that had been illegal. For that matter, with the drugs and torture techniques now available to ruthless forces in the world, Friel could be made to confess to any number of atrocities, including assassinations of foreign heads of government, whether he'd been involved or not.

Zavello knew damned well that none of his Marines had ever been involved in such deadly games. That didn't mean that torture couldn't bring a confession that would taint the entire service. And the United States.

If such a legacy were to threaten the Administration's sense of how history would regard it, the very existence of special operations might be in danger. In just months, this Administration could do enough damage to the concept of special operations and international intelligence that it might take a decade of new Administrations to overcome.

So Zavello took an electronic key to a wall safe at the front of the tactical operations center.

The safe was in plain sight of everybody in the room. It was one of four—one on each wall of the tactical operations center. So nobody could approach any of those four safes without everybody seeing them.

"Executive officer," Zavello said.

An Air Force lieutenant colonel stood up. "Yes, sir."

Zavello raised his eyebrows in exasperation. "Get your ass over here."

Zavello inserted his electronic key, and the lieutenant colonel found the slot where his own credit-card key fit. A tiny digital screen lit up on the wall, and Zavello touched a series of buttons that entered his half of the digital code that completed the operation. The lieutenant colonel entered a confirmation code. The two men stood back, and the wall safe began to buzz. The digits rolled in the window, and an audio alarm sounded.

If somebody ever had tried to open this safe, and everybody in the room had been so preoccupied as to be blind to it, the audio alarm would alert them. Now, as everybody watched—or tried not to watch—Zavello opened the safe door. When he did, a series of flashing lights went off all around the room. Another backup alert system. Reaching inside the safe, Zavello turned off the alarm systems, setting off one more three-tone alarm.

Zavello pulled out the file that he wanted and took it back to his desk. As he stepped away from the safe, another alarm sounded, warning any hands to keep clear, and the safe door slammed shut under its own power.

Zavello told himself that what he was about to do was

simply order a contingency. But it was a contingency that made his hair stand on end. He had given such an order before. Once. And it had been so much more consequential then. Now he would have to do again. Again ordering the end to the life of a member of his own Marine Corps.

Before he began searching through the codes for the one he wanted, he called out, "Winston, front and center."

Winston posted himself in front of Zavello, his legs trembling. He tried to secure them by pressing them together, and learned the meaning of the phrase "knocking knees."

Zavello looked up, his one eye glistening, glittering. Winston could not read the emotion. Was it strain? Was it anger? Was it grief?

Or was it his imagination?

"Download the infrared situation to Spartan team."

Winston shrugged. Download the situation? That's all there was? It was almost too routine. He nearly laughed in relief. He was only too happy to run back to his station to do what he had been told.

WHEN THE DOWNLOAD burst across his screen, Swayne took in the view of four clumps of thermal images. Both bands had split. The one with Friel had taken off in a separate direction. He kept his attention on the one to the east, watching Friel's PERLOBE move across the desert.

He tried to put his mind to work on the strategy of the terrorists. Keep it simple, he told himself. Don't complicate things. His enemy had simply divided so they could lay down a separate series of tracks. Maybe to confuse the Americans. Simple enough.

The follow-on group had also split. Clearly, one group was going to provide rear security to each of the original split groups. Nothing else to it.

Swayne tried thinking as his enemy. Sure, split into two forces, both still heading for the holy city. Force the Spartans to guess which one had Friel in it. If the Spartans were to split up, they would be useless as a fighting force. Even if they guessed right, the Marines would be forced to fight an enemy twice their own size, with reinforcements less than half a mile away. It made sense.

Except the terrorists would not know that Friel had a PERLOBE on him, that there'd be no guessing to it.

Meanwhile, the band that had been on their trail was just coming into view, at about five hundred meters.

Swayne calculated the timetable. There would be plenty of time to deal with these. Maybe five minutes. They did not seem to be in any tactical maneuver right now. They were just dashing forward as a group, stopping to survey the landscape, and dashing ahead again.

One thing at a time. First deal with the immediate threat.

Then jump aboard the helicopter. In ten minutes they could be repositioned well ahead of the band that had Friel. They could send the helicopter off to loiter well clear of their position.

Then, using their superior firepower and accurate weapons, dispatch the terrorists.

Pick up Friel. Get the hell out of Dodge. Deal with Night Runner's bonehead move. Then with Friel's insubordination. Simple as that.

But if things were so simple, why did he feel so ill at ease?

AZZAN'S FINGERS FLEW over the tiny keyboard until he saw the screen he wanted. A crooked smile wormed its way across his face beneath his mustache, which undulated like a caterpillar. He saw what the Americans were looking at, his four groups of men now moving toward Mashhad on two routes, the blinking signal indicating the captured American's locator beacon.

He saw the disposition of the Americans. What he

wouldn't give now for a battery of artillery or a brace of fighters to direct against them.

Even without the heavy firepower, he felt confident, though. For he could maneuver his men as if he had eyes to see through the night. Which he did, of course. American eyes in the sky.

He spoke into the miniature radio strapped to his wrist. This could be better than firepower, he thought. Using their own spy satellites to attack them. Making them lose some of that boundless American optimism. Destroying the last vestiges of their confidence.

The caterpillar looked as if it had coiled to leap off his lip.

SWAYNE DIVED OVER a low sand dune, sending up a spray of gravel. He rolled over onto his belly, his weapon at the ready. He checked to his left and right. It felt good to see Night Runner ten meters away, his focus on the approaching terrorists. Even at that distance, Swayne could see the knots of muscles in the gunny's jaw. Had it not been for his stunt, the team might already be on a helicopter. They might already be getting out of the country. Or else, they might have gotten clearance to attack the terrorist group that had wandered into the battle zone. They might have been fighting a group of professional killers instead of the amateurs who had died tonight. They might have—

Get it out of your head, he told himself. Quit ragging on it. Nobody could rewind the calendar now. They had a problem to solve. Bitching wouldn't feed the cat. Blaming wouldn't cure the ache. Only rational action would make a difference.

He gathered himself. Focused. Vowed not to let himself be distracted anymore.

He glanced to his left. Five meters away, Greiner had kept his focus, too. He was a good kid. He would work out. They definitely needed somebody to stick on this team. It had never occurred him that now they might have to replace Friel. For that matter, Night Runner might—

No. *Damn!* There he was, doing it again.

Swayne didn't want to deal with that, didn't want to imagine his Force Recon command without the Blackfeet warrior from Montana.

Besides, he had seven terrorists to deal with first.

As they closed to within three hundred meters, Swayne realized that the soldiers were not as reckless as he had first thought. Yes, they were advancing quickly, even running across the desert. But not carelessly. One flank would move forward at a full run, while the other flank would slow to a walk. It was a kind of sidewinder rattlesnake movement, one that Swayne had never seen. Whoever had developed the tactic had put some thought into it.

Once the Marines got out of here, he was going to teach it to his team. It had merit in that it did not require one element of a moving force to stop, even briefly. Everybody kept on move. The technique was even faster than leapfrogging.

He felt a tingle of relief. Had the team kept moving toward the helicopter, the terrorists would have closed in and been within rifle range. His decision to set an ambush would turn out to be the right one.

He looked for a plan of attack. He found it at once. The sidewinder tactic did have one flaw. Namely, that the entire force, although on the move, was erect. They would be easy targets.

Or would they? Swayne realized the terrorists were not walking directly at them, were not providing stationary targets after all. They were zigzagging forward, forcing him to move his aim from left to right, rather than holding to one head-on spot.

Clever. Whoever had trained this bunch had done a good job. He was dealing with somebody perhaps his equal in tactical prowess.

He had to smirk to himself at that. Never had he believed anybody could match him. Certainly not within the conventional forces of the Department of Defense. Damned few in special operations, even among the soldiers he had met in Delta Force and the Navy SEALs, whom he respected. Still. He had never accepted that any one of those units had a commander better than him. Among the foreign special-operations forces, he had met some sharp officers, and he had met some tough ones. Still, nobody to top him.

He had not even considered that anybody in the Third World military forces, even among the best terrorists, could approach his abilities. Until now.

He did remember two missions ago, when he had been left alone in the desert while Night Runner went after the Bedouin tracker who had moved around in the night like a lethal ghost—almost as lethal as Night Runner himself.

He knew he couldn't match a Night Runner or that Bedouin in the field at night. Yet he had never considered that anybody could top his ability to command a small unit under fire. He could tell that he was not dealing with an amateur here.

He did not have to give instructions to his team. Even the fresh kid knew the drill they had practiced for just such a tactical situation. Night Runner would open fire on the enemy to his flank. Greiner would begin at the opposite end of the advancing line. Swayne would take the middle. Simple as that. At two hundred meters, Swayne felt a tingle at the back of his neck. Something was amiss. The terrorist force, while advancing, had also begun to spread out.

One man at the center of the formation kept his head down, following the tracks. Unlike soldiers in an amateur unit, the rest of the formation did not collapse toward the center, where their guide had been posted. They kept stretching wider. That meant they'd be harder to take out with the boomers. There'd be survivors of the first burst of fire.

Swayne felt uneasy. He had committed himself to triggering his ambush at about 150 meters, easy range for his weapons, equipped as they were with night sights.

That was where the boomers had been laid too. But now his enemy had spread itself so wide that the boomers would be far less effective. He tried to remember how he had placed them. One was on the top of the dune, at eye level if one of the soldiers took cover there. The other he had thrown into a depression in the sand. That would be a place where an amateur soldier would dive to hide. He doubted anybody in this group was going to be hiding.

The terrorist band, spreading ever wider, was now about 180 meters out. Swayne checked the right and left flanks of the line. He saw that Greiner had shifted to a secondary position already, one that let him cover their flank. To his right, Night Runner had turned his body in position to keep an eye on the most distant soldier on that flank. Swayne's mind refigured the situation. It didn't add up.

The terrorists acted as if they expected an ambush. Deploying on a wide front made it hard to focus fire. It also gave them room to maneuver, gave them the ability to sweep toward Swayne's attack position after shots were fired. They might even close a loop around the Spartans.

Swayne did not doubt that his team could handle even twice the number of attackers that now faced them. But he could not help but admire their ability. Their tactics. And their courage. Only a well-trained soldier with a strong backbone could move into the face of a certain ambush as these men were doing.

Swayne decided to trigger his ambush early. He did not want to learn any more about the novel approach of these terrorists. He wanted to dispense with them. Because a clock kept ticking inside his head. Every moment he de-

layed here meant another few meters distance between the
team and Friel. Besides, Swayne began to suspect another
motive from this band of seven that he now faced. They
had slowed to a walk. They all walked now. All crouched.
All swerving from side to side as they came on. Swayne
saw their forward movement was slower and more deliberate. Laterally, they began to dash from spot to spot,
making it hard for the team to hold an aim.

Did they know the team's position? He checked back
and forth in his night-vision goggles. No. Nobody in the
group had night-vision devices. Was this a tactic to delay
the ambush? Were they just gaining time so the rest of
the group could escape with their captive?

Swayne wrestled with that notion. How could they
know? What if they now began taking up firing positions
of their own? What if they would now become lions instead of gazelles?

He was tempted to check out his screen. He wanted to
confirm that the band without Friel had continued toward
Mashhad. He wanted to be sure that nobody was circling
around to his six o'clock. These men made him nervous,
unlike any he had faced in the field.

He resisted checking the screen. If any such thing had
been happening, the tactical operations center would have
alerted him. Winston would have spoken up. Or Zavello—

Then again, Zavello had not said anything about a terrorist band of two dozen men materializing out of nowhere either.

A voice far to the back of his head began to sound a
warning. Somehow, this enemy had caused him to begin
doubting himself. And his support in the command operation center. Self-doubt could be even a greater enemy
than three or four times the number of soldiers he now
faced.

So Swayne made his move. He laid the aiming point

of his night sight on the man in the middle of the formation. His thumb worked the safety off, and he rechecked the aim before speaking.

"Take them."

Night Runner and Greiner both opened fire before he did. They had been waiting. They had been tense. Perhaps they had heard him shift his weight. Or seen him lean into his weapon. Or maybe they just fired at the first word from his lips.

The effect was the same. Two terrorists sprawled across the desert with the first burst of fire. Swayne, startled by the abrupt reports of the rifles beside him, found he had to reposition his rifle, and as he did so, his target lurched to the side, the side away from the track of Swayne's muzzle. Away from Swayne's stream of bullets.

Missed.

Swayne pulled back from his position and moved sideways to his right five meters, taking up his secondary position, selected in advance. To his right, Night Runner had already moved and begun firing a second burst. By the time Swayne got into his secondary position, Night Runner had already begun choosing targets from a third position. Greiner had begun shooting from his secondary.

Before firing, Swayne surveyed the landscape. He saw three bodies.

Three lousy bodies?

No, he should have been glad. To wipe out nearly half of an advancing force at the opening burst was nothing less than a success. But he had expected to get them all. Time after time, the Spartans had done just that. On the last mission in Kosovo, for instance. And earlier this very mission, when they destroyed an entire terrorist camp.

What kind of soldiers was he facing? What kind of leader had prepared them to such an extent that they could survive an ambush set off in their faces? With a survival rate of greater than fifty percent?

It took only a moment for him to realize that he had yet again misjudged his enemies. Because nobody on the opposing force was wasting ammunition shooting wild. Geysers of sand erupting in front of him told him that the gunfire was aimed low. Once again, his enemy moved up a notch in Swayne's respect. These men had been in battle before. Only pros could keep to such a strict fire discipline, keeping their weapons low so that they had a chance to kill somebody with ricochets. Huddling behind cover and firing without looking was the trademark of the green soldier, shooting into the sky over the heads of the enemy, merely making noise.

After their first reaction to the ambush, the terrorists began shooting from multiple positions. He counted at least ten. That meant that the attackers were too cautious to stick their heads up from the same position after firing the first time. Somebody had trained them at least as well as Swayne's Force Recon team.

No, he chided himself. No way.

He dismissed the notion that these were supermen. Yes, they were good. Still, they were not Force Recon Marines.

Yes, they knew how to fight—Swayne ducked as a spray of bullets came his way snaking across the desert.

As he went down, he caught a glimpse of two terrorists up and running at him. Yes, they were brave.

Amazingly so. Nobody could dismiss the courage it took to attack in the dark. Swayne saw that the bullets stitched past him to his right by at least three meters. He hardened his own will and took aim on one of the two attackers. When he opened fire, the bullets struck first in the leg, then the hip, then the abdomen. Swayne held in the trigger down through a second burst as the man fell. Right into the second spray of bullets. Headfirst.

Overkill. Friel would be disgusted. Friel, who prided himself on one-bullet-one-kill.

Swayne swung his rifle toward the second terrorist. But

his newfound respect overcame the intention. He ducked instead as a volley of return fire tore up the sand beneath the spot where his face had been.

Swayne rolled to his left and, keeping low, dove into the first position he had occupied. Once again that voice spoke to him, and he did not stick up his head. Rather, he moved off to the left a few feet farther. As that first position was showered with another burst of gunfire too.

These guys were good. They had memorized the location of Swayne's first firing position. They knew how to fight, both on a physical level and a cerebral level. They knew how Americans would fight too.

"Don't move back into any position you have occupied previously," Swayne said, to warn his men. He decided the team should find a new spot. "Two, move laterally. Pick a position big enough for all of us."

"Roger."

"Spartan One, this is Eagle 45B, check the download on your screen."

The kid with the Bronx accent in the tactical operations center. What was his name? Winston.

Swayne took a moment to heed the alert. When the small screen on his handheld computer lit up, he saw the disposition of the attacking force. He felt slightly ashamed that he had not thought to ask for an overhead view himself. But not so ashamed that he would not use this one. And now.

The screen showed Night Runner moving in an arc backward and to the right flank. That would put him in a position to support the team if the terrorists continued to press their attack. To his left, he saw Greiner near to being taken on by two terrorists. Both had set up positions. They were lying in wait. If Greiner were to open fire on one, the other—

"Four, this is One, hold what you have. Pull your head back and keep down until you hear the boomers."

"Four, Roger."

Night Runner also spoke up. "Two, Roger."

Swayne didn't like the idea of an even battle. Not for a minute longer. He pulled out his remote-control unit. Not for a second longer. He pushed the button, setting off the boomer that he had placed in the bottom of a hole.

He could see on the screen that none of the terrorists would be in a position to be hurt any more seriously than a ringing in the ears. That didn't matter so much. He needed to turn the tables on them, to whittle down the numbers, even if only by a single soldier.

The explosion seemed remarkably small to Swayne, who had used boomers inside buildings and on the open desert before to get his team out of a jam.

But that wasn't the point. He inched up to see how the terrorists had reacted. A mixed bag. One man had leaned back, exposing his head and one shoulder. A second man had merely turned his head. The third, Swayne could not pick up.

"This is Two, I have a bead."

"Take him."

NIGHT RUNNER WAS fighting the battle of his life. Not against three lousy terrorists. But inside his own head. He had to keep control of his emotions, his thoughts, his runaway anxiety. He had lost one of his men. Not in the sense that they had lost Perfect on the previous mission. Or Gunny Potts on the one before that. But in the sense that he had spent a man to teach him a lesson.

And earlier. The captain could not complete his sentence: *"If we can't get him back—"*

One word neither of them had mentioned was the one that came to mind now, *murder*. If the terrorists were to kill Friel, Night Runner would be guilty of the murder. He had set him up. He had staked him out. All that had been missing was the anthill. All that—

Get a grip, he told himself.

He called upon the spirit of Heavy Runner. Heavy Runner himself had made a fatal mistake. It had cost him his own life. He had trusted somebody, a white man. More accurately, a white man's paper. He had walked out onto a frozen river in Montana in January 1878, the temperature forty degrees below zero. He had held up the paper to show he was a good Indian. Somebody had shot him through with a buffalo rifle. He had died on the ice. The band had been scattered. Nobody took care of Heavy Runner's body so that he could reach the afterlife with the proper ceremony to prepare his spirit for the trip to the Sweet Grass Hills for cleansing, thence to the Cypress Hills for eternity.

From Night Runner's point of view, he could see only the head wrapping of the terrorist. Another wave of shame washed over him. Moments before, he had told Swayne that he could take out the man. If he had shot on the instant of Swayne's approval, that would've been the case. But he had been too busy trying to get control of his firing sequence—his breathing too ragged, his aim too tense, his pulse too rapid—to squeeze the slack from the trigger. Though it took only half a second, the terrorist had ducked backward.

Night Runner saw the head turning. The man was trying to find his companions after the explosion of the boom. For all he knew, he might be alone.

Night Runner felt his confidence ratchet up a notch. He kept his rifle sight glued to a fold in the man's head dressing. The head twitched. He was calling out to his companions. He was afraid of being left alone.

Night Runner smiled.

For the first time this evening, the enemy showed a sign of stress, a break in discipline.

A fatal break. For the man moved backward from his position and stood up. The hill gave him cover from the front, but not from Night Runner's lateral angle. Night Runner squeezed only the slightest bit more on the trigger. He saw the round take the man in the face. The head flew back, the turban flying like a roll of toilet paper thrown at a football game from the stands.

Two left. They had destroyed five of the enemy. It wasn't enough. It would never be enough, whether they killed a thousand of these terrorists. Not if they lost Friel. Not for the reason that they would be losing him.

"Spartans, get your heads down again."

Night Runner did not hesitate.

A second explosion rocked the night, this time sending debris singing overhead. The second boomer had been on a small ridgeline. If anybody had been looking in the direction of the first explosion, he would now be blind.

GREINER RAISED HIS head in a different spot, a position that he had not used before. Because Night Runner had just fired, he assumed that one of the terrorists was down. Night Runner, like Friel, always hit what he aimed at. Greiner would like to have that reputation someday. For now, all he had to do was be a good Marine. So much was happening. He didn't understand what the captain was up to, except that they had stopped to fight. He liked that part. He wasn't crazy about running away. And he wasn't too happy about leaving Friel, much as he didn't like the man.

He spotted a movement to his left. He adjusted his position one more time and made a one-word report: "Banana." At once, he felt stupid. It was a good enough word, a B-word, the code that told the others he had an enemy in sight, contact imminent, a force that could threaten but was one that the team could easily handle. *Banana?* What had he been thinking? He could have said Bison. Or Badger. Bastard even. But *Banana?*

Not that it mattered. He could see the man, evidently

blinded by the blast of the concussion grenade, stumbling laterally to get away.

Greiner raised his rifle. Two quick shots. Both in the back.

Without delay. That was how they had taught him. Just because a man turned his back on you was no reason to hesitate in this kind of fighting. This man, or a man like him, had killed seventeen sailors and four Marines on the U.S.S. *Cole*. Before that, he had very likely parked a car full of explosives outside a tourist attraction. Or set off a fire bomb inside a bus. Worst of all, tonight he and his buddies had taken a Force Recon Marine prisoner. You didn't let stupid sentimental emotions get in the way of killing somebody like that.

Greiner made his report to the team. "One more confirmed kill."

THAT LEFT JUST one, thought Swayne. One more. For a moment, he wondered whether they ought to simply try to pull out of this situation. Leave the man behind. It did not seem likely that he would attempt to follow them. One against three Marines? Not likely at all. Especially after seeing six of his mates gunned down.

Then again, one man with a rocket-propelled grenade or a heat-seeking missile could put the team out of commission. Just a well-placed rifle shot could bring down a helicopter and earn the terrorist equivalent of the Medal of Honor.

No way would Swayne sell these guys short.

Swayne had began to feel the itch that came when he knew things were moving too slowly. He hated the itch. The itch wanted him to rush, even to take chances. No shortcut was going to be worth the risk of losing anybody—anybody else—on this mission.

He made two quick radio calls to get things in motion. It gave him a chance to get his mind on the move. To be thinking ahead. To be putting together a plan for getting Friel back instead of sitting back and waiting for the enemy to act, then react to that.

He and Greiner took turns pulling out of the position. He would like to move the sidewinder of his enemy. But now was not the time to try something untested. So he and Greiner overlapped each other, moving slowly at first. Then, as they ducked clear of the area and were protected by a ridgeline, he began moving down a wadi toward the helicopter landing zone, leaving the situation in the capable hands of Night Runner.

They were capable hands, weren't they?

He chided himself for doubting Night Runner. So the man had made a mistake. So far, the worst thing that happened was the temporary loss of Friel. And that's all it was. Temporary.

NIGHT RUNNER WAS glad to be left alone. He always liked it better when he didn't have to consider the weaknesses of his mates. Yes, they were Marines, but they were still white.

He bit off that attitude. That warrior's arrogance had gotten him into trouble already.

He gathered himself mentally as well as physically. Now he was in a position to strike at the enemy, the last soldier in this bunch. He let Swayne and Greiner get out of direct fire danger from the terrorist position. Then Night Runner began swinging in a wide arc.

When he himself had gotten clear, he began to run, true to his name. Faster and faster he ran, moving laterally across the battlefield. Moving in the direction of wind. So that when he made a left turn and began cutting back toward the original ambush, he could use his nose to test the crosswind and pick up the enemy's scent. Within seconds, snatches of the breeze brought him the smell of blood and guts. He was not so sensitive that he could distinguish the smells of dead men from those of live ones. He knew from the breeze an exact bearing back toward the enemy. So he adjusted his course to continue getting to the rear of where he estimated the last soldier would be. Now there was only one thing left to consider. The surviving terrorist would either be running back toward the rest of the band, or he would be trying to track Swayne and Greiner. Either way, Night Runner was going to be behind him.

The static in his headset startled him. "Spartan Two, this is Eagle 45B."

Night Runner did not respond. He found himself crossing a ridge, and needed all his senses to detect and counter any of his enemy's moves. He had no time for chatting with Winston in the tactical operations center.

Positioning himself just below the crest, he began moving on a track that would cut the track of the surviving terrorist—if he had chosen to abandon the fight. As Night Runner went, he kept testing the air with his nose. And because his confidence had been shaken, he put his night-vision devices to use. As far as he could see in any direction, the soldier had not run away.

The soldier was a warrior. He admired that. He would die bravely. Night Runner's next move was to turn left again, completing his circuit and following a line parallel to the team's original escape route. When he estimated that he had reached a point abreast of the ambush position, he moved slowly but deliberately, counting bodies. He wanted to be sure that he had his numbers right. No more stupid mistakes for him. Not after the huge error that had lost Friel to the team. In seconds he had counted to six. He had found a single set of tracks leading away from the second kill zone.

But not back toward the safety of his comrades. Following the Force Recon team instead.

Night Runner shook his head in admiration. This was

a brave man. Going after a Force Recon team that out-numbered him in bodies, weapons, and technology.

Once he had a fix on the man's course, he slid off the track. It would not do any good to blunder into the back of the terrorist. Night Runner stayed downwind, the trick that he had learned two missions ago in that other terrorist country, Iraq.

Crabbing sideways part of the time, jogging from shadow to shadow, moving and checking often for his enemy, Night Runner hoped he was moving fast enough to catch up with the man. He heard Swayne tell the helicopter pilot to stay well clear until he gave his signal. Night Runner knew that fuel was soon going to be a factor for the Stealth bird.

Night Runner paused a moment in the night shadow of a boulder. Ahead of him, he had to cross a flat wadi, covering maybe 150 meters. He checked in both directions with his night-vision goggles, careful not to be so focused on the terrorist he was shadowing that he would expose itself to another enemy force that he had not considered. Both directions were clear. He decided to cover the whole distance in a single sprint.

"Spartan Two, this is Eagle 45B."

Damn! The kid back in Quantico had a hell of a knack of butting in at critical times.

Later, thought Night Runner. He would respond to the interference from higher headquarters after he had crossed the wadi. Then, much later, he would handle the situation in the debriefing. That much chatter had to be dealt with.

As he took off, he had not gotten more than ten strides before it hit him. The scent of sweat. Strong sweat. Too strong. From a diet of highly seasoned foods and too few baths in the desert, where water was too precious.

And the static in his earpiece again.

Night Runner put on the brakes and reversed his course.

Even before Winston spoke up, the tremor in his voice apparent even halfway around world: "Spartan Two, he's on to you."

Just as an automatic rifle opened up thirty meters away, slugs boring through the space where he would have been had he kept running.

A second burst sent chills up his spine as the air crackled behind his head. He dove and rolled, coming up behind the protection of the boulder as a third burst sent sandstone chips flying.

Night Runner had no time for beating himself up over his mistake. His enemy had revealed himself. The man, as if taking a page right out of Night Runner's book, had moved off Swayne's trail in a downwind direction. He too had stopped on the near side of the wadi, unwilling to expose himself across that distance. He had probably been sitting there wondering whether to take the chance, summoning his courage, when Night Runner ran out in front of him like a deer into the headlights. His reactions had been quick. If Night Runner's instincts had not been quicker, his night of battle would be over.

Night Runner turned his back to the boulder and sprinted away, keeping the cover between him and his enemy. He knew full well that the man would not stay in position after shooting. That knowledge gave Night Runner a slight edge. When the man took up a secondary position, Night Runner would be ready to spot him.

Keeping the terrain between him and the spot where he knew the terrorist must be if he was now trying to sneak up on him, Night Runner sprinted again, this time upwind of the man. He chose a spot thirty meters beyond. A place where the breeze was in his face. A position that would not be given away by his own body odor. He crept over the edge of the ridge, searching until he saw his man. Like the shadow of a cloud on the desert floor. Perhaps ten meters away. On the move.

Crawling toward him.

Night Runner felt a splash of astonishment. The man was acting as if he were watching the action from the—

"Eagle, this is Spartan Two," he growled into his boom mike. "Cut off the satellite download. ASAP. Acknowledge."

The surveillance satellite. The terrorists had taken Friel's handheld computer. They had figured out how to work the download screen.

What the hell is taking them so long to respond? he wondered.

Night Runner couldn't call again to ask. The man had closed the space between them until they shared the same boulder, about the size of a backyard toolshed.

The warrior dropped to all fours and began creeping around the stone, moving counterclockwise. If the terrorists wanted to peek into America's high-tech world, he'd give them something to look at.

Some things the satellite could not do.

For one, it could not hear as well as the ears of a Blackfeet warrior. Night Runner detected the tiniest of voices, somebody speaking from the bottom of a mile-deep well. His quarry had an earpiece to receive radio instructions. And somebody had just reported Night Runner's latest move.

The terrorist could not know that Night Runner heard him get to his feet to begin running around the boulder to get to his rear. Now if only—

"Spartan Two, this is Eagle Four-Five Bravo, the downlink is off."

Night Runner sprang to his feet, shucked his combat pack, and propped it at the base of the huge stone. Then he dove clear of the boulder and lay flat, looking over his rifle.

The terrorist came into view, running, waving the muzzle of his AK-47 in front of himself.

Night Runner saw the man stutter-step, as if he might skid to a stop like a cartoon character. The voice in his ear had just told the man that the download had been lost.

Either the terrorist would reverse himself, or he would try to get to his American prey in one final burst of speed.

He hesitated only a second, then rushed ahead. For the first time, Night Runner felt a moment of satisfaction. He could read his enemy's mind, understand his thinking, predict his actions. The man thought that one instant of electronic blindness wouldn't make that much difference. He could still get to the American if he hurried.

So he ran.

He saw the pack, a spot of mottled darkness against the stone, and opened fire. The pack toppled. A shout of triumph filled the night, and the man spoke into his sleeve. His excitement told as much as his words. He had a confirmed kill on one of Satan's best—

A gasp interrupted the report.

The terrorist whirled to check his six. He ripped another burst of fire into the night.

Night Runner again read the man, this time pure emotion. Fear. Panic.

He ran around the boulder in the opposite direction, firing three more bursts.

Gasping, he came back to the pack and bellowed into his sleeve, no longer worried about embarrassing himself. Now he just wanted to live a while longer, maybe to see his wife and children one last time. His fear had reached the pitch of hysteria.

It occurred to him that his enemy might have climbed the rock. So he shot into the air, sending ricochets spinning, whirring, yowling skyward off the sandstone.

All his hysteria focused on the rock. While Night Runner lay in the open, his only natural protection the dust on his desert-pattern cammies. The man knew for a certainty that his enemy hid on or behind that rock, so even if he had looked Night Runner's way, he would not have seen him begin to get to his feet.

The night went silent. The AK-47 had run dry.

The man began to fumble at the pouch on his belt.

"Don't bother," said Night Runner.

The man leapt backward, away from the voice, into the boulder. The rifle fell, and he did not even try to retrieve it.

He took a step, as if to run away.

Night Runner swung, feeling the wounds across his back even as he inflicted a wound on his enemy's neck.

The man's momentum carried him forward another two steps before he sprawled, silently bleeding out into the desert floor. His head, separated from the rest of his body, bounced over a pile of stones, becoming one with them.

Night Runner drew a deep breath as if he might shriek his war cry in triumph. But he did not. There would be no triumph until he had recovered the Marine that he had as much killed. No peace until he had brought Friel back from the dead.

He unwrapped the turban from the head and melded with the shadows. In case one more terrorist lay in hiding. He would not repeat a mistake he'd made on his last mission.

He wiped his blade clean. Thought about taking the man's hair. Dismissed the idea. He had taken his head.

It was enough.

SWAYNE HEARD THE automatic gunfire. Several bursts. He knew Night Runner had not fired his BRAT automatic rifle. The sound was from an AK-47.

He tried to analyze the situation. All those bursts. No report from Night Runner. That wasn't necessarily bad. He could be too close to the man to utter a sound. The terrorist might be throwing shots at shadows, although that did not seem likely after what he had seen from these fighters.

He touched his mike button. Then stopped himself from saying the words. What if the sound of his voice in Night Runner's earpiece might alert an enemy close enough to hear? No, better not let Night Runner know that Swayne had doubted him for a second. All these missions. All Night Runner's work performed to a superhuman degree.

Now, after just one error in judgment, and Swayne was ready to doubt him.

No, he would not. He insisted that he would not.

"This is Two. The trail is clear."

Swayne controlled his sigh of relief so that his radio mike would not pick it up and betray it to Night Runner.

He called to the helicopter pilot, and Night Runner advised him that he would circle the position until the helicopter set down. He was going to make sure the area remained clear, to warn them in case any other enemy soldiers had picked up on the sound of gunfire.

AZZAN LEFT IT to the sound of gunfire and explosions to tell him how the battle had gone for the band of soldiers he had sent after the Americans. He hoped they had spent their blood well, to gain time for him to escape with the prisoner.

Azzan and the rest of his soldiers had made up an hour's time. Perhaps they were three miles closer to the holy city. Once they were there, there would be safety. They could hide themselves. Or else they could disperse. And they could hide their prize.

The handheld computer had flashed once and faded to black as he followed the fight. So. The Great Satans facing him weren't the dumbest Americans he'd ever faced. They'd figured out that his quick countermoves meant he was using their own tools against them. No matter. He had tools of his own.

He put his mind to evaluating the night's events. So far, except for being too obvious about using the tiny computer map, he had played the Americans perfectly. They had stayed in character. They had followed the tactics he knew they would. He had pricked them, and they had flinched. He had pushed them, and they had fought back in an ambush. He had taken his captive away, and they had not thrown themselves into a fight against his delaying forces.

Those things told him what he wanted to know. The special-operations soldiers were dashing toward a pickup zone. They would either flee his country or try to pursue him in a helicopter.

He smiled. If they vanished like curs, he would have his prisoner. If they came after him, he might have more than one.

ABOARD THE HELICOPTER, the cold night air failed to chill Swayne's anger. He gave the terse report to Zavello and supervised the distribution of ammunition from the on-board supply stores that went on every pickup bird for just such an occasion.

This helicopter ride should be one that took them out of the Iran. They had pulled off their mission, just as it was briefed. The enemy intrusion would not have been a factor. They could have been clear of Iran if not for—

Swayne had to stop stewing about Night Runner's mistake. Grant the man one damned mistake, he told himself. Wait until you return to garrison to hash it out in the debriefing. By then, Friel will be in hand.

Swayne did not want to think about the alternative.

WINSTON, IN THE Operational Mission Command Center, had laid down the track of the remaining terrorist bands on Swayne's computer screen before the signal had been interrupted. Swayne saw them moving on diverging tracks away from the original strike zone. Both had set courses to Masshad. That he could not permit. Once they had Friel inside a city that big in an area so remote, they would have little chance of getting him out. Several things might happen to Friel, all of them bad. He might be taken by helicopter to Tehran, where he would have to deal with the Ayatollahs. Or he could be held in the outlying holy city until this or some other terrorist chief came on the scene to explore new ways to exploit the captive. Not a good possibility. The terrorists would want to extract everything that they could from Friel, including the last bit of his dignity, before killing him.

Swayne had dreamed of running into a terrorist leader face-to-face someday. He had visualized how he would take apart a ruthless killer like—

Azzan!

What the hell was wrong with him? He had just spent the better part of two hours fighting a force that was uncanny in its discipline and tactics. Yet the possibility that he might have been facing Azzan's troops—and even Azzan himself—had not even crossed Swayne's mind. Before the attack, he had been focused on how worthless the mission was going to be. Then, when he was in the middle of a fight with a force that was anything but routine, he had not even considered that he might be facing ultra-elite troops trained—and led—by the American-schooled Azzan.

He keyed his radio mike. "Eagle, this is Spartan One, can you give me an analysis of the possibility that we could be facing Bin Azzan?"

The duty officer who answered was not Zavello. "This is Eagle Niner. Reports indicate that is a negative possibility. Azzan's last known location was southern Afghanistan. There is no evidence—"

"Belay that. This is Eagle One." The familiar snarl of Zavello rasped the airways. "We have no more idea where

Azzan is than Eagle Niner has a chance of finding his own ass with both hands."

Swayne was glad to hear Zavello's acid voice. It calmed him to know that somebody so decisive was still at the switch in the operations center.

"Why do you ask the question?" Zavello wanted to know.

Swayne gave a quick debriefing, matching details from the night's fight to what he had seen in the pre-mission plan.

Before this mission Swayne had more than once studied the full bio on Azzan. He had pored over pictures of the terrorist dressed in his traditional Arab garb, in a military uniform, and in street clothes as a student at the Command and General Staff College at Fort Leavenworth, Kansas. He had tried to get into the head of the man behind that closely cropped beard. He had asked questions, first and foremost: Why would somebody with all his wealth, coming from a history of comfort and convenience, turn to killing innocents?

Most Arab princes he had heard of were much more likely to risk their lives getting mugged in New York after a night of partying. Or driving the most expensive cars in the world too fast and too drunk.

But here was a killer who had put himself on the world's most-hunted list. Intelligence services kept on the lookout for the man and his signature tactics. Very likely, he could never sleep in the same bed twice. The cash rewards for his hide were so great, it must have been difficult even to find enough people within his own circles to trust. That's why they were so well trained, of course. If they were not loyal and dedicated and smart, he would have already booted them out of his gang. And nobody could leave a gang like that in possession of his own life. You either made it with Azzan's band or you didn't. If you made it, you could never leave. At least not alive.

The reward posted for each member of the terrorist band was so high that even Azzan's family had to consider it worthwhile to betray him. Only fear kept most of them from doing it.

Anybody who tried to make Azzan's team and failed could not be allowed to live either. That was why Arabs joked darkly that whoever signed up with Azzan was on a one-way ticket to heaven.

Swayne studied a preprogrammed map on his computer screen and picked an ambush site. He pointed it out on the aircraft commander's navigation screen.

He avoided the obvious. He wanted no part of high ground overlooking terrain that would channel the band. A unit like Azzan's would send out scouts to screen the flanks and trigger the ambush before the group guarding Friel ever got into range of Swayne's strike. Instead, he picked a spot two miles farther to the northwest. It was a large plateau, at least twenty kilometers wide, with a dry wadi snaking across it diagonally. Because there were no distinctive ambush sites better than any other there, sending out scouts to check out terrain features would be pointless. If anything, scouts would simply set a screen a couple hundred meters away from the main force and march parallel to it.

So Swayne decided to spring an ambush of opportunity on the band that had Friel. He would tell the pilot to drop the team beyond the dry streambed, and take up a vantage point to watch the approach of the terrorist band from afar.

The streambed would give him the edge he needed. The terrorists would have passed through miles of ideal ambush terrain. Each time they cleared a wadi or skirted a rock pile or hillock, they would grow more nervous. Finally, when only the wadi on the plateau remained an obstacle, Azzan's men—even if he stayed behind with them, prodding them—would relax. They would stop assuming the worst and begin to assume the best. They would think the ambush danger had passed because the landscape no longer lent itself to ambush.

Then Swayne's trio, lurking beyond the wadi and staying well clear of any screening force, would let the terrorists pass. The Spartans would dash up behind the band and strike them from the rear.

Swayne felt his belly lift as the helicopter began a descent. He checked the digital navigation map one last time before touchdown. Everything on track. His pilot had selected a route into the area that had taken them low-level on the zigzag, generally due east. At the last moment, the pilot had taken a sharp turn northward, and was on a high-speed approach.

Swayne slapped the backs of his two men—Night Runner flinched, sucking air, and Swayne wondered: *Had the gunny been hurt?*

Swayne gave the hand signals. Greiner and he would leap out one side of the craft, and Night Runner would exit from the other, as soon as they felt ground contact. With their night-vision goggles in place, they could be assured of not jumping into a desert badger hole or on top of a spiked plant.

The tail wheel touched first and pitched the cockpit forward. Even before the front wheels were down, the Spartans bailed. The sudden loss of weight helped buoy the aircraft into its takeoff. Swayne looked up and saw the aircraft bank on its right side, heading back toward the east. Then again toward the north. And back to the east. Swayne liked that. He was working with professionals. If somebody were tracking them by night-vision devices or radar, things that probably did not exist in this part of the desert, they would have the impression that the aircraft was on an aimless search of the desert floor. They had not been in this spot more than three seconds before the team was off. Chances were good that nobody had spotted them touching down.

Unless they were within fifty meters. Which was why they moved quickly to clear the area. Night Runner hunched over and darted out of sight. Greiner followed. Swayne remained at the site for a moment, providing security, checking in all directions before clearing the area himself.

Everything on schedule. Once they had made a hundred meters, Night Runner worked his way toward the gentlest of swells in the sand to look out over the plateau toward the east. Swayne showed a series of hand signals to Greiner, and made his way up to look toward the west. He saw that Greiner found a spot in the shrubbery where he could look to the south. They had formed a triangle, the shape of the fortifications the French had used in Vietnam. No matter which direction the enemy appeared, at least two sets of eyes and two weapons would be instantly available for recon and defense. So far, not a word had been spoken. So far, not bad.

Swayne checked the situation, reviewed the new mission, reconsidered the execution, weighed the logistics, and rehearsed the command and signal aspects of the operation. Satisfied that every element of the five-paragraph field order was in place, he went about looking for his enemy.

After he satisfied himself that the area was clear, he briefed the team in a low voice over the air so Zavello could hear too.

Then he asked himself: Did he feel a momentum swing in his favor? Yes. He had gotten over his snit about being thrown into a mission in which the only enemy had been a bunch of high school dropouts. His doubts about Greiner—doubts that he would have had about any new guy, no matter how well he performed in training—had been all but erased. In every situation, the man had shown composure. No flash. No excess of emotions, neither exuberant nor fearful. Brave, but not reckless. He had handled himself well under fire. He had directed his own shots carefully so that every bullet counted. As raw material, Greiner had already proven that he would stick as a Force Recon Marine. Give Night Runner a few more weeks to put some finish on the guy, and the Spartans would be whole again. Unless . . .

Night Runner. The man had showed Swayne something that he did not think existed. Night Runner had proven himself to be mortal. He had made an error in judgment. A serious error, to be sure, one that tainted the aura of perfection from Swayne's mind.

As he scanned the horizon with his NVGs, looking for the enemy, Swayne had to admit that the new reality was a good thing. He needed to see Night Runner as somebody like himself. Somebody who had faults. Somebody who had doubts. Somebody who could make mistakes. Now he would get a chance to get a new measure of his gunnery sergeant. In the cold, stark light of reality instead of the soft glow of hero worship. Night Runner was a good man, yes. Emphasis on *man*.

He rubbed his chin, thinking that—

Wait. He was smelling a familiar, muggy scent. Blood. He sniffed his fingers. Definitely blood. He wanted to flash his penlight on his hand to check, but knew he could not resort to that rookiest of rookie errors.

Mentally, he inventoried his body. Nothing. No pain or sting. No feeling of cold wetness, except under the straps of his combat pack.

He remembered patting his men on the back in the aircraft. Yes, one of them had been wounded.

Not Greiner. He would have reported it, not to complain, but to let the team know its effectiveness might be diminished a notch.

Night Runner. He'd been hit in the ambush. He would

have kept his mouth shut. He would never have complained as long as he could function. Especially not after his mistake in losing Friel. Night Runner had been hit. He was keeping the injury quiet.

Swayne deliberated. Best to leave it alone, he decided. Pull off this ambush. Recover Friel. Call for the extraction. Forget the rest. The rest was nothing but distraction.

Still, he'd have to talk to Night Runner about this business of hiding a wound from the team. What the hell was wrong with the man?

NIGHT RUNNER HAD already checked his area of recon responsibility and cleared it a dozen times over. As he expected. He turned back to look over the captain's shoulder. Literally. Swayne lay behind the crest of the small knoll, looking in all directions with his night-vision binoculars.

Night Runner had never felt so much pain. Not merely because he had lost a man. But because he had perhaps thrown away the life of a man. He felt sure he could recover in the captain's eyes. But how could be ever get back Friel's respect? He had treated him like an expendable life. Friel was no Blackfeet warrior who deserved to be condemned to an ancient test of courage. You couldn't tie a white man to a tree at the edge of the forest and leave him to face the grizzly.

As Night Runner had faced the great beast himself.

He flexed his shoulders and felt the searing reminders of the experience across his back. He knew by the chilled spot that the wounds had opened, that blood had seeped across his back, staining his desert camouflage beyond the extent of the pack.

AFTER THE LAST mission, in Kosovo, Night Runner had found his way to the summer camp of one of the most respected elders, a medicine woman, small, frail, and somber. Alice Walks with Bears.

He found her in a sparse camp on a gravel bar beneath Swift Dam at the edge of the Blackfeet Reservation. She sat tending an Indian's fire, tiny but smokeless, cooking a fish on a stone beside the stream. He stood off at a distance respectfully, not wanting to intrude, unwilling to startle her. He took in everything he could with all his senses.

A fickle breeze wafted mist over the camp from the dam's spillway, a giant fire hose at the base of the concrete. The cold mist and hot sun took turns embracing him, first chilly, then hot. The torrent roared, muffling the sound of the forest, but overhead a hawk spoke to him.

He looked up and felt the bird's shadow flicker on him. He looked down to find the shadow blur its way across the landscape and touch the shoulders of Alice on the way by.

Only then did she look up from the fire. Into his eyes. No surprise showed on her wizened features. She nodded as if she'd known he was there all the while, at the same time giving him permission to approach.

He did, seeing that the campsite was nothing but a camo military poncho stretched and tied to saplings, her bed a simple scooped-out place in the pea gravel. He saw a rolled wool blanket, Army issue, and a boning knife. Nothing else. Members of her family had told him where to find her. They'd said she had been out for three weeks. Night Runner wondered how she had survived with so little. He knew Force Recon Marines that would not have done so well. Friel, for one.

She was dressed in a simple calico dress, a common red bandanna around her neck. Her brow sagged over her eyes so only glittering slits showed. Her face was patterned with deep creases that crossed each other, forming diamonds of skin.

"Hello, Grandmother," he said in the language of the Blackfeet, hoping that he wouldn't be asked to say more, to reveal one of his cultural shortcomings. He knew the white man's language better than most of them. But he didn't know his own people's language as well as many white men.

"Hello," she said in a strong voice, in English. "Sit, and we will eat this fish together, hey?"

Night Runner suppressed a smile. A trout that small wasn't going to sustain her, let alone him. But he would not be rude. He sat and waited for her to speak.

"You look like kin to Heavy Runner," she said.

He could not contain his astonishment. "How—?"

She smiled, giving him a checkered look of mischief. "I seen you playt the basketball at Heart Butte, hey? I know you from the newspaper and the yearbook. You ain't as skinny as back then. The Marines, they feed you good."

"Yes, Grandmother."

"Alice. I like Alice."

"Alice then."

She deftly peeled back the skin and flaked pink meat off the trout with her boning knife. She offered it to him with her fingers.

He took it in the palm of his hand and waited for her to take a portion. As she began to eat, he spoke up.

"I came to—"

She shook her head. He shut his mouth. They ate the fish in silence. He savored the delicate flavor and wished he had a slab of it to eat.

Afterward, she said, "I know why you come. Nobody your age come to me at my home unless they want to beg money for that goddamnt whiskey, hey? And nobody your age come to me here unless they want to beg for stories. You want stories, hey?"

"Yes."

"I am a keeper of stories, you know. I am raised by my grandmother, who told me the stories of our people. I keep them and tell them and pass them on to my own granddaughter." She turned her head and picked the white hair of a fishbone off her tongue. She wrapped the fish remains in a square of foil, as if she would save the skin and bones for later. "What kind of stories you want?"

"I want to know about the warriors of our people. I want to know how they prepared themselves for battle, how they found their courage, how they—"

She raised a hand. "You been around the whites too long, hey? You talk too much."

Night Runner felt himself blushing. He'd always prided himself on being a man of few words. Among white men, he supposed he was. Here, he was a blabbermouth, like one of those radio jocks who can't keep their yaps shut for fear of dead air.

"You want courage, hey?"

"Yes," he murmured.

She snorted. "I can't give you any damnt courage."

Night Runner began to wish he hadn't come.

She said, "You already have the courage. I seen that in your eyes before you said a word. While you were standing there before that hawk brought us together. It takes courage to ask about courage."

She leaned over and picked up her blanket roll. She sheathed her knife and the foil packet in the roll and clutched it to her chest.

She shook her head. "But you're an Indian." She pronounced it *Indin*. "You're a hardheaded Indin that won't take my word for it. You want to prove you have the goddamnt courage the Indin way, hey?"

"Yes, Grand—Alice."

"Even if it kills you."

He didn't answer, so she answered for him. "I suppose.

Better'n letting the damnt whiskey kill you. Come on, I'll help you find your courage."

She gained her feet before he could offer a hand to help. He followed her into the forest.

She led him to a meadow bathed in sunshine. She plowed a path through waist-high grass toward a stunted pine in the middle of the open space, about two hundred meters in diameter. She marched at a good pace, he thought. She'd make a damned good Marine.

At the base of the tree, she turned on him. "You don't have to do this, Night Runner."

She hadn't told him what it was he'd have to do. But she was telling him now that it would be dangerous. He didn't care. He liked it that she called him by his Indian name instead of Robert. "I want to learn, Walks With Bears."

She didn't object to her Indian name. She stared at him, the slits of her eyes all but closed.

"Listen, Night Runner. You have the courage. You come here to prove what you already know, what I already seen in you. But you want to do this Indin thing to prove what you already know. I'm telling you that even if you prove it, it could kill you. You die a hero? You die a cowart? What the hell's the damnt difference if you die, hey?"

He narrowed his own eyes and knew at once the answer to her question. "If there's a difference, I'll know it."

She shrugged and put down the blanket roll. With a flourish, she uncoiled its contents, leather strips the size of boot laces, three foil packets, and the knife.

"Get undressed," she ordered. "Even your shorts."

He did as she ordered.

"Stand closer to the tree."

He did. She brandished the boning knife.

"This is going to hurt," she said.

He nodded, feeling giddy that they had begun this rite

of antiquity, knowing he would never relent now.

She knelt next to the pine and picked up two six-inch green pine stakes freshly cut and sharpened at both ends. She turned to him, her mischievous grin a bit more wicked than before. She had known he would come here, that he would not be denied. She had prepared for his passage along an ancient path.

"Give me your back, you stubborn damnt Indin."

He saw by the look in her eyes that she was fond of him, that she did not want him to die in his quest for courage.

He felt her pinch the skin on his back and pull. Then the knife sliced a hole through the skin between her finger and his back.

It hurt, all right, but not as much as he'd expected. In any case, this would not be the test of courage anyhow.

That would come later. In the night.

SWAYNE SHIFTED HIS position. In the distance, perhaps three kilometers away, he saw movement. He calculated that the terrorists were moving in a straight line. At a jog. A slow jog, to be sure, because they were slowed down by one man stumbling between a pair of guards. Swayne grunted into his boom mike. When the others turned toward him, he pointed.

NIGHT RUNNER SAW Friel. That pole was still thrust between his elbows. He should have been glad to see that the man was capable of moving under his own power. He realized he would've felt worse if they were dragging Friel. Or even just carrying his head as a trophy. They should not have been in control of a Force Recon Marine at all. He had even cheated Friel out of the dignity of fighting to the death.

Their route would take them past with about two hundred meters clearance. About right for what the captain

had briefed. The element of surprise that would give them
the best chance to recapture Friel.

How could he ever face Swayne again? How could he
remain in Force Recon? If Friel died tonight, whether at
the hands of the terrorists or after taking a bullet from the
team, it would be his fault. It would be murder. Would
Swayne turn him in?

No, he would not. Night Runner would not allow it.
Night Runner would not force that decision on a superior.
He would confess his crime. Take his medicine. Take the
court-martial. Take the dismissal from Force Recon Marines. Do his time. Go back to Montana, and disappear.
Perhaps find his atonement at the clearing. Washed clean
of his sin by a final act of suffering. Absolved by pain.

He thought he had known pain. At the meadow where
Walks with Bears had left him in the long shadows of
afternoon.

THE MEDICINE WOMAN had sliced him twice through two
folds of skin, making four slits in his back beneath his
shoulder blades.

She did not tell him what she was doing, but he knew.
He could see the process in his mind's eye. She threaded
a green pine stake through each pair of slits, then looped
an end of the leather thong over the points of each stake
and pulled it tight, snubbing the loop beneath the stake
against his back.

"Kneel," she ordered. "And back up until your feet
touch the tree trunk, hey?"

She stood behind him and drew the thongs back and
up like cruel reins. She fastened them to the eight-inch
trunk of the pine.

"Try to stand up then."

He did, leaning backward to reduce the pull against his
wounds. He felt blood oozing down the backs of his legs.

He was naked, except for the medicine pouch on a beaded thong around his neck.

"Try to turn around to untie the knots."

He tried, but as the thong on one side gave him slack, the other tightened. "I can't reach around to untie the knots," he said, the tone in his voice letting her know she'd insulted him by suggesting it.

She ignored his petulance. "You can stand. You can kneel. You can't lie down. You can pray. You can cry out. I won't hear you. I won't come, no matter what, until morning."

He looked at her without blinking.

"Okay then. You have showed me proof enough of your courage. There would be no damnt shame if I cut you loose now. Or do you want me to pray over you, hey?"

He stared at her.

She shrugged and began speaking in the guttural tones of their language. He recognized only a few phrases. "Great bear" was one that ratcheted up his pulse.

From a fold in her dress she pulled a pouch, a stone shaped like half a baseball, a knot of grass, and a Bic lighter.

Forgetting his pain for a moment, he watched as she dampened the knot of sweet grass in her mouth, lit it, and placed it into a half-inch, perfectly round depression in the flat side of the stone. She held it close to her face as she prayed, using one hand to fan the smoldering fire, letting the smoke carry her words skyward. He inhaled the acrid sweet grass, the incense of the plains.

Once the embers flickered out, Walks With Bears never hesitated in her ritual, never stopped her musical chant. From one foil packet, she took a piece of the trout skin and pressed the oily side into the stone depression. Rubbing the oil into the soot with two fingers, she made a greasy, black paint and smudged a design on Night Runner's cheeks.

She avoided eye contact, as if he were a condemned man. Only once did she hesitate, before wiping the fish skin over his chest, on his belly, and on his thighs.

At his feet, she placed the open foil package of fish remains. Half a step farther away, she put the second foil packet down and opened it. He saw it was a mixture of nuts and seeds. Beyond that, she placed the third packet, revealing dry fruit.

Finally, she stood before him, one long, crumpled hand outstretched.

"Give me your medicine bundle."

He made no move to take the small pouch from his neck. "It's my medicine, my shield against harm."

One corner of her mouth lifted in scorn. "If you need protection, I'll bring you a rifle then, or a goddamnt condom, hey? What did you come here for anyways, Indin?"

To test his courage, of course. He had to do this without a talisman. He removed the bundle and gave it to her.

Not appeased, she hissed at him. "Here's your protection if you need it." She dropped her boning knife within his reach. "Pick it up and fight when the bear comes. Or cut yourself loose and run when you hear him snorting in the grass, hey?"

He squatted, finding his knees had grown stiff from standing under the tension of the pain in his back. He grasped the knife and handed it toward her, handle first.

She shook her head. "Giving me the knife is not the way to courage, hey? Keeping the knife is the way. You think about it, Indin with the blood of Heavy Runner. And tell me tomorrow how that can be so."

SWAYNE'S VOICE BROUGHT Night Runner into the here and now.

"Spartan Two, this is One. Let's move it."

Night Runner realized by the clipped tone in Swayne's voice that he must have been talking to him for some time now. He found yet another reason to feel shame. He had allowed his focus to dissolve. Swayne had caught him in the act of reliving his daydream.

One quick sweep of the landscape told him what was going on. The terrorists had begun crossing the wadi to the north, a kilometer away. They had done it right too. He saw two one-man patrols just climbing out of the depression, traveling behind the main group. Two other men flanked the band about a hundred meters ahead of the group and the same distance to the side. They weren't going to make it easy. At least, not for a normal fighting unit. The men in the screening patrols could sound the alarm and trigger a fight if anybody tried moving in. Two other men would be free to come to their assistance after they fired the first shot, moving in from at least two directions.

Night Runner joined the captain at Greiner's position for an updated briefing.

Swayne told them how to implement his plan, now that they'd seen the enemy disposition, wasting no words. Night Runner was to take down the security force. He and Swayne would then attack the main body to free Friel. Greiner's job would be to stand off, keeping the remaining two scouts from joining the action.

SWAYNE LOOKED AT Night Runner and saw the knots in his jaw and temples. He could not see into his eyes because of the night-vision goggles. It surprised him that Night Runner would use them at all. Usually, he relied on his own vision instead of the high-tech devices. But after the way things had gone, maybe he had doubts about his own ability. Just as Swayne was doubting him. He realized the moment had grown awkward with him staring at Night Runner. It wouldn't help the man's confidence.

Now was not the time to speak up about why the gunnery sergeant had gone to sleep on the radio either.

Swayne nodded. Then he blinked, and Night Runner was gone. His night-vision binoculars showed a tendril of dust where the man had been. Nothing more. Swayne shook his head. He looked at Greiner, who was checking the space around himself, even more confused than Swayne.

Swayne led the way, crawling out onto the plateau. Keeping low, he used his night-vision binoculars at 20-power to locate the nearest scout. A little more than a half mile away. Now walking with the rifle slung over his shoulder. On the horizon, the lights of the holy city glowed, no more than a handful of kilometers away. The terrorists were nearly home, and had passed the last best place for an ambush. The terrorists were now thinking that they were within range of a reaction force from the city. No more than a few miles to go. A few miles to go before they slept.

Swayne motioned to Greiner and began walking at a brisk pace, trying to close the distance to the scout, knowing that the man would not see him with the naked eye at this distance. Now that Night Runner was on his trail, the terrorist did not have long to live anyhow.

NIGHT RUNNER MOVED fast, running as much to burn off his anxiety as to close the distance between himself and the terrorist.

He had stowed his goggles and microphone. With those things not strapped to his head, Night Runner felt more like an animal of the night than a man.

This was more like it. This was the state of a true warrior. He could hear the sounds of his footsteps. The soft-soled boots were doing their job. Giving him a feel for the earth. Traveling across the crusted sand almost without making a noise. Unlike the hard, sharp-edged boots of his companions. Even better than the sandals of the man he was following. For now he could see that he was in the tracks of the man.

By the stride, he could tell that he was closing quickly—one of his running strides covered two of the terrorist's. The toes continued to point forward, and outward at about ten degrees. The man was strolling now. Confident that his group was safe. Not once did the tracks show a deviation, a crumbling breakup of the soil picked up and tossed by the shoe of a man turning his head, shifting his weight to look over his shoulder. The man had spent all his caution. It would cost him his life.

Eventually, Night Runner made out the figure. He had closed almost too quickly.

As Night Runner closed to within hearing distance, about forty meters, it made no sense to stop and reconsider an attack strategy. He simply made one up on the spot as he closed to within twenty meters.

He unsheathed the sword he had picked up in Iraq two missions ago. On the plains, his ancestors might ride by an enemy and swing a tomahawk. It was the white man's cavalry that used the long knives. He would play both roles.

Ten meters. Without breaking stride, he raised the blade to his shoulders. He did not decide yet whether to pass by on the right or left. He would leave that decision to the scout.

Five meters. The man had slung his rifle over his right shoulder. Night Runner went left.

Three meters. Night Runner put his free hand to the right side of his mouth and hissed, directing the sound to the left. As if it were coming from the desert faintly.

One meter. The man, not yet hearing the footsteps, turned to the left and started to bring down his rifle. It never left his shoulder.

Night Runner planted his left foot, jogged right, and

swung the scimitar. It caught the terrorist high on the head, above the ear, slicing through the cloth, hair, skin, skull, soft matter.

Night Runner kept running, barely breaking stride. He glanced back over his left shoulder and saw the top half of a melon hit the ground and roll in a circle. Just before the body struck, skidded, and came to a rest. All without a sound. The man had gone to his heaven, scalped in the most efficient way. Night Runner had taken the scalp of his enemy before. In the desert of Iraq. Not to keep. But to offer up to the spirits of his ancestors.

About two hundred meters ahead walked another scout, grown just as careless as the previous one. A scout who would die as quickly.

Night Runner repositioned the earpiece for the moment. Just long enough for him to make his report and to hear whether Swayne had any changes in the mission so far.

SWAYNE HAD BEEN watching. It had happened so fast. His attention was on the terrorist soldier as his body merged with a shadow coming up quickly from behind. The night-vision binoculars had amplified the shine of starlight on metal, and the blade had seemed longer and broader as it swept its arc through the air. He saw the man go down. Night Runner began to close on the lead sentry. Now Swayne and Greiner had to speed up. They had fallen behind because Night Runner had moved so swiftly.

Swayne understood Night Runner's haste came from his anger. Now, if only it did not make him careless.

In another few minutes, Swayne slowed to a walk and motioned for Greiner to close up. In the field, they would normally never walk side by side. Here, with Greiner at his right shoulder, they would appear to be one man if somebody observed them from the left. The post of the walking scout would seem to be filled. He made the snipping motions with his fingers, and they both shut off their mikes. He told Greiner to hold the spot. Then he took off running after Night Runner.

Just as Swayne thought he should be catching up to Night Runner, he topped a gentle rise and saw another terrorist corpse sprawled in the sand. Night Runner stood waiting for him.

Night Runner whirled to face Swayne, his Iraqi sword cocked, the flash of the instrument carving a Nike swoop in the heads-up display of Swayne's night-vision goggles. Even as Swayne raised a hand, he could see the hatred draining from Night Runner's face.

Swayne acted it as if he had not felt threatened, and flipped his left hand in the direction of the terrorists. "Have you seen how the main body is situated?"

Night Runner shook his head, as if to bring himself back from the edge of a third kill with that scimitar of his. "Negative, Captain. Last I looked, they were still moving, still hauling Friel along. The kid must have a hell of a headache. Yet he keeps up."

"He's a Marine."

The small talk done, Swayne and Night Runner studied the group. Swayne had briefed that they would take up the positions of the scouts and gradually close in on the main body, as if the scouts were simply drifting off course. He had seen earlier in the night that this group of men was not disposed to making mistakes. But it would be worth a try, since the group was so close to Mashhad and feeling comfortable by now. Let the leader of the band chew him out. For the last time. His last reprimand.

Night Runner walked so he and Swayne made the profile of a single man to the main body of the band.

Swayne checked the landscape with his binoculars, examining the winding highway that made its way toward the holy city. The terrorists were on a line to intercept the highway. The Marines couldn't allow that to happen.

The terrorists might have trucks ready to pick them up,

an escort that might add more weapons to the mix. Or a stray military vehicle might happen by once the Marines began the attack. So it was important to catch these men by surprise in the desert, pick up Friel, and call in the helicopter, which was now sitting down, engines off, vulnerable but conserving fuel. Once they launched it again, the craft had only ten minutes left on station before it had to return.

Besides, they had to get Friel soon. Dawn was less than an hour and a half away.

GREINER STUMBLED ACROSS the desert floor. He tried keeping his eyes on the scout at the rear left of the main band, a quarter mile away. He tried to keep track of Night Runner and the captain too. Which divided his attention just enough so that he could not spend much time watching where he was going. What amazed him was how well the senior men were able to move in the darkness. Here, he had one of the most sophisticated set of night-vision devices in the world, and still had trouble walking without looking down at his feet.

He could see elements of the main band in front of him. The captain had told him to drift closer to the scout on the far side, the better to have a clean shot. He'd better make it good too. The second scout on the far side would react from the front left of the terrorist band, either going directly to the aid of the first scout, attacking the source of the gunfire, or reinforcing the main body.

The captain had told Greiner that couldn't happen. It was imperative that he knock down the first man and move immediately into position to off the second man.

If he could do that, he was to move into position where he could lay down fire on the main band. By then Swayne and the gunnery sergeant would have the terrorists under fire. Greiner should be able to get some clear flank shots. His job was to make sure that he did not, first of all, shoot

Friel. Second, to make sure nobody in the terrorist band decided to take out the captured Friel.

It seemed funny. After all the crap that he had taken from Friel, part of his job was to save Friel's life.

Greiner rehearsed throwing down on the scout. When the landscape allowed, he would drop to one knee, sit back on one heel, and take careful aim. No problem hitting the man in the center of mass. Friel always bragged about his head shots. Greiner would not rise to those taunts. A body shot would accomplish what he wanted. Knock the man down. Finish him with a second shot, if necessary. Get into a secondary position. Take on the second man. He looked for him. Still, he could not find the man walking left flank for the terrorist band. It nagged at him.

The main band was easy enough to see. He brought his rifle up and took turns picking them off with imaginary shots. Of course, none of them would stand and wait for a second shot after the first guy took a header.

He remembered to watch where he was going just in time to avoid strolling through a clump of trees laced with thorns. He detoured around the growth and checked the open area for his scout.

First his heart stopped. Then his feet. There was nothing to see. No scouts. No terrorist in the main band. Suddenly, the entire situation had changed.

That was not fair, was it? The captain had told him what was going to happen. Now nothing was going to go down as the man had said.

What kind of bullshit was that?

No wonder Friel had developed such an attitude.

SWAYNE AND NIGHT Runner caught the signal at the same time. Both hit the ground. Swayne could hear Night Runner's rifle go off safety, even as he pushed his to the automatic-fire position.

"I'll watch the main body," he said to Night Runner. "See if there is anything on the highway." He laid his scope on a man seated in the desert. No cause for alarm. The terrorists were simply taking a break. Somebody from within the main body had flashed a penlight in all directions. Elsewhere on the landscape, the scouts would be expected to sit down out of sight and maintain security. Or else close up on the group for new instructions. Perhaps change positions with somebody inside the main body. There was no way of knowing. So he had to keep watching. If anybody left the main body, so much the better.

It would mean the terrorists were swapping scouts. A replacement for each scout would leave the main body—and meet an untimely end. The main body would be expecting another man to come back in to the group for each one that left. If that man happened to be a United States Marine, well, too bad for the home team.

Only one thing could go wrong. If Greiner were somehow to miss the penlight signal and be spotted. Swayne rolled onto his side and checked the landscape where Greiner should be. Nothing. That was good. The kid had caught the signal. He had stopped in place.

Swayne turned onto his belly and saw two of the terrorists ambling his way, obviously looking for the men they would substitute for on the flank. He murmured into his mike, "Spartan Four, stay put."

Swayne nodded to Night Runner, who slid off their dune like a shadow, moving in the direction of the terrorist pair.

Swayne kept his night-vision goggles in place so he could keep a fix on Night Runner. Even at that, he was afraid of losing contact with the Blackfeet warrior, who—

"Spartan One, this is Eagle One, over."

Zavello. Again, with the uncanny timing, speaking up when Swayne wanted least to hear from him. Swayne saw

Night Runner drop to the ground to hold in position, knowing that Swayne would not want to be talking while Night Runner was trying to sneak up on the flank of the terrorists. Night Runner's body language betrayed his disappointment, more a sagging to the ground than a tactical move.

Swayne knelt and acknowledged the radio call. Then, as Zavello began relaying his message from higher headquarters, Swayne felt his own shoulders droop. He sat on a heel, then lay on his side.

Zavello demanded an acknowledgment, then demanded it again.

Swayne could barely say the words. "This is Spartan One. Wait, over."

He went to his computer, preloaded at Quantico. He found the codes menu and used the numerical instructions from the one-eyed colonel to access a maze of other menus that could not be browsed without the keys from Zavello.

Then, when he'd arrived at the final firewall in the handheld computer, he reported, "Spartan One ready to receive."

A satellite transmission from halfway around the world activated an electronic key, opening the last door. Swayne entered his personal code, hoping that a computer glitch would end the chain of events now set in motion. Maybe he could fake it. But the computer gave him the reply that authenticated the receipt of the message. Swayne repeated the words: "Wilco, Scenario five-seven-seven," barely able to say the words.

Zavello signed off.

Leaving Swayne feeling eviscerated. Make that betrayed and eviscerated. By his own kind.

What was it, one Administration and several missions ago, they'd been ordered to kill the kidnapped Commandant of the Marine Corps if they couldn't rescue him?

Afterward, when he'd had the ear of the Commandant, Swayne had made the case that a field unit should never be put in that position. The Commandant had argued the case to the highest levels of the previous Administration.

But that was aeons ago by political standards. The brave new world had a brave new Administration. An Administration that had to establish itself as tough. That called for tough measures.

Friel would be the recipient of those measures. Friel, if he could not be rescued, was to be assassinated.

Swayne knew that Night Runner would be watching him. He made a fist, pointing with his thumb, and gave the knocking signal that told the gunny to move out. The gunny hesitated, and Swayne knew why.

STUNNED BY SWAYNE'S words, Night Runner crept forward. Again, he would be in the lead. If the scouts spotted him, he would stumble and fall to the desert floor. He would cry out as if he had twisted an ankle or a knee. When the terrorists let down their guard to mock him, he would come at them from the flank. With his sword.

That would leave only four men in the main band. No matter. In his state, he could handle six men. Twice that. No matter what it cost in terms of his own blood or that of the terrorists he was going to save Friel. *Scenario five hundred and seventy-seven, be damned*. There'd be no assassination. At least not by him. He would die trying to save the man he'd condemned to this fate. When this entire operation was over, there'd only be two options. If he lost his life in the effort to save Friel, at least he'd be vindicated by the spirits who had power over him in the afterlife. If his own spirit were allowed to migrate to the Cypress Hills of Canada, the place of the afterlife, the great warriors would welcome him for an honorable effort.

If he succeeded in saving Friel, he'd have to deal with the White Man's power. He was willing to take their punishment. He could deal with the physical pain and shame if they should imprison him. He could handle the disgrace if he were to be drummed out of the Marine Corps. He could go back to a solitary life elsewhere on the planet, somewhere in Montana or where he did not have people to depend on him, where he did not have to depend on others.

The one thing Night Runner could not bear would be the death of Friel because of his own stupidity. Even in the Cypress Hills, he would be marked by the shame of it.

It took all of Greiner's willpower to avoid becoming a spectator. He saw Night Runner closing on the pair of terrorists in the distance, Swayne bringing up the rear. How he would have liked to watch them operate. He could learn so much just by watching the Indian move. How he could glide from shadow to shadow, sometimes even drifting out of sight in the night-vision goggles.

Greiner was not supposed to be a couch potato in this action. His job was to take on the scouts in his sector at the rear of the terrorist band. So he had better spot them and do something about them. He scanned the horizon, looking for the two men, first the near man, then the far. Still nothing.

"Eagle 45 Bravo, can you give us a body count and disposition of the band we're now moving in on?"

That Swayne. Thinking of a solution to Greiner's problem, as if he were inside his head. The man was always ahead of everything.

"Roger," said 45 Bravo, the radio operator Greiner had never met, a man who had become a part of the Force Recon team by being the overhead eyes and ears.

Winston reported that there were still five bodies in the main group. Four terrorists and Friel, whose beacon still identified him.

"And I have a fix on the Spartans," Winston said. "Plus two in the vicinity of Spartan One and one other bandit to the northeast of the main body."

Greiner shook his head. There should have been one other terrorist.

"Check again," Swayne ordered. "Look for a bandit to the northwest of the formation. Spartan Four needs to know where that scout is."

Greiner was glad to hear the urgency in the captain's voice. Because he did not have to betray his own anxiety. He was supposed to take the man out, and he did not have the first clue where to find him.

Until the man spoke up, not two meters away, calling out to Greiner in his language. From the sound of the voice, Greiner was about to get a good old-fashioned Arabic ass-chewing.

Except that the surprise of having the man pop up in his face caused him to clutch that trigger of his rifle and stitch the terrorist with automatic fire from his groin to his neck.

NIGHT RUNNER STILL seethed that the Marine Corps would order them to kill one of their own. Marines should not have to—

The gunfire from Greiner's position rattled the stillness of the night. Night Runner recognized it as an American rifle even before Winston's shaken voice confirmed that Greiner had taken out the missing terrorist.

Followed by another report from Winston: "Spartan Four, be advised a bandit is extremely close to your position."

Night Runner spat. That was what staff people were good for. Telling you what you already knew long after you really needed to know it. In a situation like this, even a couple of seconds later was far too late.

But that no longer mattered. The element of surprise

had been lost. He and Swayne had not been ready with rifles aimed, and the two nearby replacement scouts were no longer standing. Like any soldier, they'd dropped to the ground so they could avoid being targets. Next, they'd be looking for targets of their own.

He did not blame Greiner for opening fire. It was the right thing to do because his enemy was so close. So close, in fact, Night Runner had heard the terrorist's voice activate Greiner's microphone.

No, Greiner had made the right move. Only an old hand would have done anything else, such as attack with a bayonet. Or that scimitar Night Runner had.

No matter now. Now he and Swayne had to act.

As if on cue, Swayne's voice filled his earpiece. "Two, I'll cover the scouts. You take the main band."

A surge of relief swept over Night Runner. The captain, sensing his pain, was letting him make the attack that would undo his mistake, the move that would free Friel.

He raised his rifle and fired, sweeping the rest area of the terrorists. Naturally, they had all flattened. And, of course, Friel lay prone too. Night Runner could see him, his face buried in the sand, his elbows pointed upward because of that pole crammed through the crooks of his arms behind his back.

Gunfire answered both from the camp and from his right rear, where the scouts had taken cover. He never even looked back. The captain—

A burst of six brought a cry from one of the scouts. That Swayne.

Night Runner came up in a secondary position and focused his night sight on the band to make sure none of the four terrorists there was making a threatening gesture toward Friel. Next, he picked one to eliminate. The largest of the four targets. A single shot to the eyebrow made the body shudder and go still.

Next, without seeking a new position, he decided on

the most dangerous terrorist, the one lying beyond Friel. The man had positioned himself to use the Marine's body to shield himself from Greiner's direction. But that exposed him to Night Runner's aim.

Night Runner lowered his sight past the top of the man's head wrap, dropping down three inches to make sure he would hit skull.

Before he could pull the trigger, the captain shot, and the man's head cloth flew off into the night like a night hawk.

Damn! Night Runner thought. They had lost a second by aiming at the same terrorist at once. Their shots might have killed two of the enemy. Instead there were now four alive, two in the band and two outside. One scout on the near side and another on the far side. Neither could be allowed to rejoin the main body or shoot into the group to take out the one American, the captive one.

But all of this was a waste of time trying to figure. He needed to select a secondary target. He chose the man to the right of the clearing, who had not yet exposed himself. All Night Runner could see was the heel of one foot. Good enough. The man would be in such pain he might not be an effective fighter.

Night Runner heard bullets snapping by and ricochets singing into the night around them.

He squeezed off the shot. And adjusted his aim to where he expected the rest of the man to be when he reacted to being hit. The foot flattened. The back arched. Night Runner waited until the head and shoulders came up, and fired a burst of three, a tight shot group between the neck and the ear.

Night Runner rolled once to take up a secondary position a scant few meters away. Even in so quick a move, he found that things in the kill zone had changed. A lot. To his surprise, three terrorists were up and running away.

Had he lost count? Had one of the scouts joined them?

No, Friel had somehow freed himself and was escaping into the darkness too.

Night Runner took aim at a second man, but before he could pull a trigger, saw bullets slapping into the man's back. Swayne's bullets, raising dust, leaving craters in the fabric of his jacket. Half in anger, Night Runner squeezed off a burst at the last man from the main body. He couldn't see a result, but knew he'd missed. That was what happened when you shot in anger. It hardly mattered now. Now the momentum of the mission had swung their way. Now his blunder did not seem so huge. Now Friel had broken free of his captives.

He and Swayne had the same idea at once, and were both up and running toward the enemy. Friel had headed east. The terrorists had run straight away, to the north. Whether Friel was now crawling on his belly, his knees, or had hidden out behind a rock or nestled into a hole, they had gained an edge. Friel had put some distance between himself and the bad guys. Night Runner and the captain sprinted through the darkness, never exchanging a word, both knowing they had to get into the space the terrorists had created by running. Put themselves between Friel and the enemy. Bring the kid from Boston back into the fold, end this nightmare for him. And for Night Runner.

The two terrorists left alive would not be a factor. If they kept running, they might live to tell this story. If they did not try to recover Friel, they could survive to tell their story or to make up a new one for all Night Runner cared.

If only there was a way to tell them, *Go home. Stay away from our man. We will let you live. All we want to do is to take our own back to his home.*

But of course that would never happen. He knew from the caliber of soldier they had been facing, from the fighting they had already been through, that there would be no fleeing. This fight was far from over. The pair left alive might be desperate, even running away in panic. Eventually, they'd resign themselves to their certain deaths—their terrorist leader would not let them live if they ran from a fight and gave up the American prisoner so easily. Even if they knew they could not defeat the legions of the Great Satan that had routed them, they would come back to fight, seeking everlasting glory, dying to get to their heaven.

Night Runner reached the edge of the kill zone first, and detoured wide to pick up the track of one of the men who had run from the area. He did not follow it very far, just far enough to make sure his man had not made a circle to the right to take after Friel. Once again on this night, he had to struggle to control his emotions. The last thing he needed now was to get careless because he was overcome with joy at the prospect of pulling Friel—and his own ass—out of the mess he had created. Yet he could not dally. If that man caught up with the psychotic sergeant—

SWAYNE DID NOT follow Night Runner beyond the kill zone, but veered to the north so he could be in position to react to any of the terrorists who would turn back on Friel and try to recapture or kill him. Once he cut Friel's track, he settled in to look in all directions for his own man and to be sure that nobody else was trying to sneak up on Friel.

He made a brief radio call to let Night Runner know that he had secured the area. Nobody was going to get to Friel except through him. He also called to Greiner, to bring him into the fold. He didn't want another man left out to dry. Not now. Not when they were on the verge of success here.

GREINER KNEW THAT the main ambush had probably drawn the attention of the remaining scout. Which meant

Greiner was out in the middle of no-Marine's-land with no mission. So he was glad to hear Swayne call him in. His first instinct was to bound to his feet and get on the move. But he had watched the members of this team. He had learned to fight down the first instincts. Especially those that came from the gut. First instincts made you reckless. First instincts could get you killed.

So he scanned in every direction before moving out of his alternate firing position.

Only then did he begin moving toward the area where the main battle had taken place. And then not on a direct line. Starting off on the oblique. Moving maybe a hundred meters west. Stopping, checking the area, then striking out in a different direction. Working his way across the desert without being predictable. Swayne and Night Runner would not be disappointed in him. They had hammered at him, telling him about their own mistake once in the Iraqi Desert. That had seemed so abstract to him. Nothing like a night of combat to turn abstraction into reality.

Inside two minutes, he reached the point where he could survey the battlefield. Around him lay the bodies of the terrorists that Night Runner and Swayne had put down. Without moving into the kill zone, he looked around carefully and found the form of Swayne. The captain hooked an arm at him, beckoning him in.

Greiner detoured around the kill zone. One more thing he had been told. Not to go through an area where soldiers had been shot. Not enemy soldiers, not even allied soldiers. People who were hit were in a murderous frame of mind. They might awaken from a stupor and kill the first standing person they saw. Or shoot at the first thing that moved.

Moving at an oblique heading still, Greiner slid past Swayne, taking up a position behind him so they were sitting back-to-back, providing security for each other. It was a good feeling to be paired up with one of his mates again. When he was alone in the desert and responsible for all-around security, he had never felt so lonely.

But where was Night Runner?

SWAYNE WAS NOT so concerned about Night Runner, who could take care of himself. Where the hell was Friel? He had checked in every direction and saw no sign. He felt an urgent need to get up and begin following the man's tracks. But he resisted that impulse. If Friel were dazed, he might be staggering in circles. For Swayne and Greiner to be wiping out the evidence that those tracks could give to somebody as experienced in reading sign as Night Runner would be a sin. No, a crime. Now that they were this close, the only thing to do was to wait for Night Runner to get back.

Half a minute later, just as he was becoming anxious enough to figure yet another action plan, he saw a shadow moving his way and tried to pinpoint the blur in his NVGs. The mere difficulty in getting a fix on the figure made it Night Runner, almost to a certainty.

"Coming in," said the familiar voice in his ear. It brought a smile to Swayne's face that they were within minutes of getting Friel back. He was tempted to make his radio call, to launch the pilots with the helicopter that would take them out of Iraq.

All they needed was Friel. Where the hell—

"I've got Spartan Three," said another familiar voice. Greiner. Now Swayne did smile. He turned in his spot and saw the form coming out of the night toward them.

But something was wrong. Friel was blindfolded. A gag had been placed over his mouth. Where once his arms had been freed as he ran out of the kill zone, they were now bound again. A rifle was in the crooks of his elbows.

Behind him were two other figures. With rifles.

"He doesn't seem to know where he is," said Greiner.

"Request permission to go out and pick him up."

"Negative. Keep your ass down."

NIGHT RUNNER HAD followed the tracks of one terrorist until they joined up with another. Then they had struck off on a direct line toward the north. The terrorists were going after Friel. Rather than follow them directly, he turned back and took up a heading that would intercept them before they got to the kid from Boston. Now, if only Friel would keep his butt down. If only he had not been hit too hard on the head—Night Runner felt the twinge of shame for having done that to his own man. No telling how many times Friel might have been battered by the terrorists.

When he had reached the kill zone, he found the tracks where Friel had run off. He fitted his night-vision goggles to his head so he could read the tracks and extend his distance vision. He needed to find Friel before those two terrorists.

Once the goggles lit up the night, all too brightly for Night Runner's comfort, a surreal story unfolded in seconds.

The two forms he had picked up without using the goggles turned out to be Swayne and Greiner, as he had supposed. But it wasn't anything in the troops or terrain that struck him odd. It was the story at his feet. The tracks of Friel running out of the kill zone.

He looked up from the track, and raised his rifle. He could see Swayne and Greiner in the mid-distance, shifting on the desert floor. Trying to get a clear shot at the two figures behind the man in the Marine Corps cammies.

The night-vision goggles contributed to the surreal scene. All at once Night Runner understood why he did not like them. They were too much like a vision.

And now the vision he had seen in the bear's den materialized here in the Iraqi desert. Finally he understood it. Wasting no time. Taking no chances. One finger touched the laser sight, sending a red beam slicing into the night, a spot half the size of a dime at a hundred meters. He laid the spot on Friel and two things happened at once.

Thing one, a stream of bullets flew, temporarily washing out the vision in his night goggles.

And thing two, he hoped to hell he was not going to have to explain to a court-martial panel that the reason he'd killed Sergeant Henry Friel in the Iranian desert was because he had to fulfill the vision that prophesied he would kill his own son.

SWAYNE SAW THE laser dot, red and bright as neon, plastered to Friel's chest. He knew where it had come from: Night Runner.

He expected the beam to slide over Friel's shoulder, to pick up one of the figures behind, either one. Neither one of which Swayne could get a clear shot at.

But the beam did not move. Puffs of dust exploded from Friel's uniform, and the man fell over on his face.

Greiner opened fire the instant the firing lane was cleared to the other two figures. Swayne could see them clearly now. Greiner's bullets hit one man low, and as the terrorist fell, he dropped into the path of follow-on slugs and was hit half-a-dozen more times. The kid used a lot of ammunition, but he had done his killing thoroughly.

Meanwhile, incredible as it seemed, the laser beam did not waver after killing Friel. Instead it moved onto the face of the third man. The man could obviously see the light on his nose. He swatted at it. But it was not like a mosquito that could be swept away. A burst of three slapped back, cutting through the hand, the face, the head. The man went over as if he had been struck in the head by a cannonball instead of 5.56mm slugs.

Something gripped Swayne from the inside out, a feeling of dread that he had always feared. This was it, the moment in combat that his grandfather had warned him about, the thing that would get him killed. The old man, Jamison Swayne, the Senator, crusty and bitter as the rasp in his throat. A man who had never worn an American fighting man's uniform until they issued one to him on the ship as he was sent to the forests of France in 1918. Once there, he'd had barely time enough to soil the woolen material. No sooner had he occupied a trench one night than the Germans had attacked, following a cloud of green gas lit up by overhead flares in the night.

The chlorine had taken out the old man before he had fired a shot in anger.

Now the Senator had nothing left in him that was not tinted with his own green toxic hostility. For some reason, it was directed at his own son, who had gone MIA in Vietnam, presumed dead. And his grandson, who had now done what the old man had warned he would do. He had frozen on the battlefield. He had not opened fire. The shock of seeing his gunnery sergeant kill one of his own men had paralyzed Swayne for a moment. Certainly, it was for a short moment, he rationalized. But it was paralysis. He recognized it. He cursed himself for it.

So that's what the old bastard had been trying to say for all these years. He'd frozen in battle. He'd thought his own son—Swayne's father—might have been killed by being a victim of the same genetic flaw. He did not want his grandson to be in the military. Not because he hated somebody in his own family. Because he did not want the youngest Swayne to die of the same genetic flaw that had already cost the Swaynes so much.

The insight struck Swayne so hard in the chest, he put a hand to his uniform to check for blood. Surely the impact must have come from a bullet.

Friel might have been saved if he'd opened his mouth. If only—

Night Runner.

Damn!

His gunnery sergeant had gone berserk tonight. Swayne's whole world seemed to be crumbling before his eyes. This mission, his career, his self-confidence.

But Night Runner's collapse, that might be the worst of it. First the blunder of hitting Friel. Then tying him up with the ridiculous idea that watching the battle unfold and not being able to participate in it would teach him a lesson. Then a Force Recon Marine had fallen into enemy hands. The most ruthless enemy hands on earth. They would kill Friel for pleasure. They would turn him over to Iranians in Tehran and watch Friel torn apart for the television cameras as a punishment for the night's invasion.

Face it, Swayne told himself. Night Runner had snapped. He had exercised the order to kill Friel at the very moment when it looked most likely that they would rescue him. Swayne had found a sin the man could commit. One he could never forgive.

"Greiner, go check out the casualty." He didn't have to say which one. "Gunnery Sergeant Night Runner, report to my position at once," he growled into his microphone. "Get over here. Now."

Swayne felt himself trembling with—there was only one word for it—rage. All the anger he felt toward his grandfather, all the resentment that he had not known his father, all the insanity on this particular mission, all that he had ever lost and needed. They had been focused into an emotional black hole, a force of gravity so severe that no light, no joy, no pleasure could ever radiate from Swayne again. On the last mission, he had seen Nina Chase resurrected from the dead, but changed for life.

And now. For God's sake, Night Runner had killed one of his own men. In cold blood. There was no other explanation for it. What in hell had he been thinking? That to kill Friel would relieve him of a witness to his stupidity earlier in the evening?

He felt a hand on his shoulder. He brushed it off and whirled to face Night Runner, unable to hide the pain in his voice. "What in hell were you thinking, Gunny?"

"Spartan One, this is Eagle One. Report."

Swayne tossed off his helmet and ripped the microphone from his head. He wasn't about to put up with interference on the battlefield at a time like this. He didn't care whether a helicopter came to pull them out of Iran. He would rather finish this whole affair right now. He wanted no part of going back to the comfort of the United States. Not with one of his men in a body bag. Not with this.

Night Runner pulled his own microphone off.

The two men stood facing each other, tense and stiff as two dogs sizing each other up before taking the first bite.

Greiner cleared his throat as he approached, giving them a warning that he had returned from his mission. He stopped four steps away, seeing enough in his night-vision goggles to know that something had gone terribly wrong. "Sir?"

Swayne did not even turn his head. "Shut up, Greiner."

"Begging your pardon, sir, the dead man—"

Swayne whirled on him. "Lance Corporal Greiner, do you want a court-martial too?"

"It's not Friel," Greiner whined, flinching as if he expected to be hit.

"Shut—what do you mean it's not Friel?"

"The dead man, sir. It's a terrorist. A terrorist dressed in Friel's uniform. Friel was nowhere in this bunch."

Swayne turned back to face Night Runner. A new feeling, a wash of both relief and shame. Swayne had not said much. But the way he'd said it. His tone. His accusation. Had he actually said *Court-martial?*

Swayne knew damned well that he had amplified Night Runner's blunder by his own miscalculation. He had first frozen. Then, in fury at himself, he had cut loose on Night Runner. The things he had said, once released, could not be taken back. Could not be vacuumed out of Night Runner's ears.

Night Runner had stood at attention the entire time.

Swayne refigured the situation. None of it looked good. Here he was standing in the desert facing his man as if he was going to lash out with his own rifle and club him to the side of the head. As if they were two schoolkids on the playground getting ready to fistfight. Dead soldiers all around them. A band of terrorists out of their reach. A band with Friel still in captivity.

For the first time since he could remember, Swayne was all out of ideas. He had no options. He had reached the situation that he had never anticipated.

He felt beaten.

"Shouldn't we clear the area?" Greiner asked.

Swayne's shoulders slumped. "Move out, Gunny."

Swayne thought he saw Night Runner's shoulder flinch, as if he was about to haul up and snap off a crisp salute something right out of the movies. In the field, only an amateur would pull that. From an old hand like Night Runner, it would be nothing less than an insult.

As the Force Recon Team slipped away from the battle zone, trudging more than creeping, Swayne tried to find a ray of redemption in the night's events.

The terrorist leader had trained soldiers as well as any Marine Force Recon Team. They had pulled off a masterful ruse. They had tricked the man who thought he was the smartest Marine captain in uniform. Ever.

Now Swayne had embarrassed himself and his senior enlisted man in front of a subordinate. Never in his life had he seen himself acting so stupid. Never had he imagined being defeated.

A distant voice was shouting at him. He remembered Zavello. At the end of the microphone cord, the tiny ear speaker transmitted a voice bellowing, as if Jiminy Cricket were giving him an ass-chewing.

Hell with the one-eyed colonel. He had nothing to say to the man back in the Operational Mission Command Center. Zavello was going to reprimand him anyhow, worse than any of the two thousand or so previous ass-chewings, probably in writing this time, probably for his personnel jacket. Swayne had never suffered that indignity before.

No matter how bad it was, nobody could do anything worse than he had already done to himself.

He had blurted out that he had lost confidence in his sergeant. He had caused the sergeant to lose confidence in him. The junior member of the team had stood around like a kid in the Christmas pageant who had forgotten his lines, embarrassed that he had to witness the falling-out of his only two surviving superiors in the field.

Swayne did not even feel that he could go check out the Friel impostor himself. That would be like calling both Greiner a liar and Night Runner an idiot yet again. All the while making an idiot of himself.

Ahead, Night Runner stopped, knelt, and skirted to the side about ten meters. He motioned for Swayne to close up.

Swayne crept up and knelt. His skin crawled with shame for the mess he'd made. Greiner moved into the group, sitting with an ear cocked for instructions, but looking back on their trail to provide security.

"Sir?" Night Runner said, his voice calm and professional. "Shouldn't we take the personal items out of Friel's uniform. Get anything that tied him to the Marine Corps and take it out of here? The PERLOBE and all?"

Swayne saw that Night Runner was showing him the

way out of this awkward situation. It shook him out of his paralysis.

"You take care of that, Gunny. Greiner, get out there and give us some security on the north. I'll move to the south and give a call to headquarters. Figure something out."

Greiner did as he was told, but Swayne grasped Night Runner's wrist and held him until the youngster had moved out of hearing.

"Night Runner—"

"No need to say anything, sir. I caused you to lose confidence in me. You wouldn't have said anything if I hadn't made you doubt me."

"We can get it back," said Swayne, shaking the wrist for emphasis. "We can get it all back. Respect, confidence, Friel. One bad decision. That's all it was. Then a chain reaction of breaks that went against us.

"We followed the PERLOBE because we didn't suspect they'd trade clothes with Friel. That's all. But look what happened. We finished off half the group—hell, more than that, if you count that first band that tried to follow us."

Swayne realized Night Runner had begun nodding. Yes, they had done something positive. They'd eliminated part of the terrorist force. They'd struck down one of the options their enemy could use against them. The groups divided, plus they don't know who they are—they're guessing.

Swayne released the wrist. "I apologize, Gunny."

He saw Night Runner's hand reach toward his shoulder, then pull back. An old hand like the gunny would never touch the person of an officer so informally.

Swayne didn't need the touch. He felt the gesture in his chest, where it counted.

"The chain is broken," he said to Night Runner.

"From now on, we get all the breaks," the gunny responded. He vanished into the night and returned two minutes later, taking up the chase again without a word.

As they cleared the area, Swayne felt it coming back to him. His confidence. This did not have to be a lost situation. Not if he would not let it. Things had gone out of control, yes. But that did not mean they had to spin into chaos. The team had, on balance, won every engagement so far. All that was left was to recover Friel. One simple step, he told himself, not feeling as cocky as he wanted to feel.

Of course, he was forgetting a step. Before anything, he had to strap that microphone and headset back on. Plug the tiny screaming voice into his ear, where it would grow to its most nasty, most gargantuan size. Take his medicine from Zavello. Release the helicopter. Get back on track.

He waited for a break in the tirade. Finally, Zavello stopped for a breath. Or had he coughed himself into a seizure?

Swayne dismissed the hope that his boss was having a heart attack and said, "Eagle One, this is Spartan One, I have a full report."

And the ass-chewing began.

SOMETIME LATER, SWAYNE said his *yes-sir, yes-sir, three bags full,* and put his mind to work on the tactical situation without the distraction of screams and threats.

By now he was certain that his enemy, the one that he had underestimated, was Azzan. American-trained, desert-experienced. Swayne had studied an onboard dossier on his handheld computer and felt he knew his man, a man whose goal in life was to humiliate America. He would do that by attacking targets on United States soil or around the world. He had embarrassed United States Marines in the desert. Now that he had Friel, he might embarrass the country in the global press.

Azzan had won Round One. Give him that. Time for

Round Two. Time to take back Friel. Deliver the knock-out punch.

Swayne had cobbled a plan together in his head. At a rest stop, he ran it past Night Runner. Together they brainstormed it, played the devil's advocate to each other. To all appearances, things seemed normal between them. To a new guy like Greiner, the spat had been patched up.

Swayne and Night Runner knew better. The scars would be tender for a while.

They had the mission to work out, though. The plan was a healing ointment because they had to do it together. That it seemed an impossible mission made it all the more useful as a mending tool.

Azzan had won time with his ruse of using a fake Friel, either by accident or on purpose sending the team after the locator beacon hidden inside a pen in the kid's effects. The terrorists had made it safely into the holy city with their prisoner.

That gave a twist to the mission. The Spartans had not done any city fighting, except in mock-ups and training areas. They had not tried moving as a military force through a city the size of Mashhad dressed in full combat gear. Swayne checked the sky—the glow in the east told him that they were within an hour of sunrise. Tonight, after one hell of a long, hot day, they would.

THEY WAITED FOR the day to pass in a gully outside Mashhad. Swayne had traded reports with Zavello every four hours, each time the snapping and snarling a little less vicious than the last. The gravity of the situation had forced the colonel to keep less to reprimands and more to intel reports.

Zavello needed to have information from troops on the ground, and it wouldn't do to have them beaten down and sullen. Once again, technology was proving every bit as fallible as men. Events of the night proved it wasn't enough to be able to see images moving around as green blobs on a radar screen. The spy satellite had been fooled by the terrorists as completely as Swayne's team had been tricked.

Swayne had used his time on watch to put his own mind back on track, starting with a review of events after the last firefight.

Before dawn, the team of Force Recon Marines had angled to the east to take advantage of the rugged terrain and to stay clear of major roads.

Before extracting the helicopter, the pilot landed at a spot on the main highway leading into the holy city, and took off immediately toward a refueling rendezvous and a low-level escape from Iran. Any reports to the terrorists would suggest the Force Recon Team had hit the highway, where they were picked up for extraction.

In fact, Night Runner had led his men to the LZ spot half an hour before. They'd jogged a mile down the roadway so their tracks could not be picked up when they stepped into the desert again. As Swayne and Greiner moved toward the foothills, Night Runner brushed up footsteps for a hundred meters or so away from the blacktop.

Now they lay in a ravine, sticking to the shade, both for comfort and for camouflage. They ate, napped, sweated, and waited.

Swayne felt confident that anybody who had seen or heard the helicopter would send the military to investigate. They would find a set of tracks running onto the highway. They would not find any evidence of those footsteps on the other side. Clearly, the Marines had escaped. To the conventional military mind, the danger was past.

Azzan was another matter. Swayne wasn't about to underestimate him again. He studied the terrorist's dossier again and again on the LED screen during the day.

He would know him when he saw him next. He would know how to deal with him.

Azzan became the target of his anger.

Forget about Friel's psychosis. Forget about Night Runner's lapse in judgment and Swayne's own abrupt miscalculation in doubting the best Marine he'd ever met—hell, ever heard of.

Swayne knew he could make up for all those shortcomings if he just forgot about past mistakes and zeroed in on the future. All he had to do was put Azzan in his sights and erase the past with a head shot.

MASHHAD, IRAN
1357 HOURS LOCAL

FRIEL COULD BARELY contain his rage. The ragheads had dressed him in stinking sheets, something like a saddle blanket for a camel. Or maybe they had just wrapped him in used toilet paper, for all he knew. What he did know was that he reeked.

He could feel the cooties crawling out of the turban or whatever it was, marching around his scalp, making him itch. He had cursed out the terrorists a time or two, but they had responded to him with more violence each time he opened his mouth. The first time, he got a rifle butt in the pit of his stomach. The second time, the cheese-eating leader of the pack pummeled his ribs with fists, taking his breath away for a long time. Once, after they put a rope around his neck and led him like a dog, Friel called the man at the other end of his leash a string of names that came out as a single thirteen-syllable word.

Which earned him the flat of a rifle stock across the back. It had been swung like a baseball bat, and it drove the air from his lungs and paralyzed his right arm because of a nerve it had struck in the area of his shoulder blade.

His head fell forward, and he could not raise his chin off his chest. It scared Friel to death that he could not lift his chin again. Maybe the blow had fractured a vertebrae in his spine, maybe cutting his spinal cord. For hours he could not recover his breath at all, so he knew with each jab of pain that at least one rib had been broken.

Three times was the charm for Friel. The Marines had always bitched him out for opening his mouth at all the wrong times. He snickered to himself. Too bad the captain hadn't used a rifle butt on him a couple times. This kind of treatment really made him want to keep his bean-hole shut.

But he was not contrite. He was not subdued. He had been stung. First by his own men. Now by this. But he could fake that they had broken his spirit. He could look for an opportunity to grab a broomstick, split the shaft, and park it up a terrorist ass.

Be as good a way to go as any, and it did not seem likely that he was going to survive this mission anyway. His lucky number had always been 21. It looked as if he was going to be finished before he ever got that high in the event scenarios.

Oh, yes, the Force Recon Team would be coming for him. But probably not in the sense that he wanted. He had a memory long enough to remember Event Scenario 13. Then he had been given the orders to kill one of their own, an Air Force pilot who was about to be downloaded into a Cuban submarine.

Word was that assassinations had been called off after that. That the Commandant of the Marine Corps no longer would permit any of his men to kill other friendly soldiers. Or to be killed by special-ops troops.

Right. The Commandant wasn't always in charge of shit, was he? Sometimes, politicians had the say. And politicians could make you kiss whatever parts of them they wanted. Even if the Commandant quit. Even if Zavello

quit. Even if Swayne resigned in protest. They would find
somebody else to do the shooting. They would go through
the whole list of chickenshit officers on the rolls until they
found one who wanted to jump from Marine lieutenant to
Marine Commandant, getting on the fast track by guiding
a 20mm blowpipe round up the ass of some measly sergeant out in the middle of Bumsuck, Iran.

Oh, yeah, they were going to kill him, all right.

*Gimme a broom and let me sweep the room, boys.
Which one of you assholes wants a pointed stick in the
eye?*

That sounded hollow, even to Friel. He didn't want to
get himself killed. Why give those officer lowlifes a free
pass? If he killed himself by getting into a scrape with
the ragheads, that gave the officers what they wanted.
Which was one dead Irishman. If they wanted to flush
him, let them do it themselves. Why do their dirty work
for them? Swayne wanted him dead? Let Swayne—

Swayne.

He tried to get his mind around the notion of Swayne
looking him in the eye down a laser beam. He couldn't
make the picture in his head.

Swayne wasn't like the normal garden-variety chickenshit officer. Swayne would try to find a way out. If he
and Swayne had been on the street together, Friel would
never have had to give up his life of crime—there
wouldn't be enough crime for the both of them to do.
Swayne woulda been the ultimate criminal. Smart.
Smooth. Titanium balls.

Too bad they could not have been friends. Too bad
Swayne had not lived up to his potential as a criminal,
had wasted his talents by going into a life of officership.

Officers. What good were they?

Forget officers, he told himself, riding back and forth
on a pendulum of pain in his ribs and emotion in his chest.
No officer was going to risk his officer ass for him.

Face it. He was not going to get out of Goat City now. The goat-eaters had tucked him away for all time. The best he could hope for now was to take a couple of bastards along with him on the trip to terrorist heaven.

But he would have to use his head. He would not be able to talk these bastards into anything. And he would not die old if he kept cussing them out. No, they were going to put an ice pick through his ears the next time he opened his mouth out of turn.

He was going to have to use his smarts.

One of the terrorists didn't seem to like the look on his face. The one he called Gateway, for the black birthmark that flowed out of his head rag and down his forehead like hot fudge, tugged at the rope around Friel's neck.

A bolt of pain shot down Friel's spine, sending a twenty-syllable word to his lips.

Only ten syllables got out before a rifle stock hit him on the ear, sending him reeling to the floor. As he lay on his side, trying to get the gyroscopes in his eyeballs to stop oscillating, he thought: *Oh, yeah, that was smart. Very smart.*

THE DESERT NEAR MASHHAD, IRAN
1545 HOURS LOCAL

SWAYNE ASKED, "HOW did you know?"

The day-long silence had troubled Swayne. The quiet did not come from emotion, but necessity. They had to take turns sleeping, so they could refresh themselves. And they had to maintain security by keeping somebody awake at the top end of the ravine.

Now Greiner held that spot. Swayne and Night Runner were supposed to be resting. But Swayne could see that Night Runner was not going to be sleeping anytime soon. He just sat staring at the opposite wall of the gully.

Now black sparkling eyes turned on Swayne. There was no hostility in them. As if they had been carrying on the conversation in fact instead of in their heads, he said, "The tracks. I saw the tracks and knew they were not Friel's."

Swayne shrugged. *How?*

"Henry's boots, yes, but not his track. I could tell they were on somebody else. They were too big. The Iranian sloshed around in them, and the track they left was not like anything I had ever seen from him before. If we had hit that track earlier, I could have told you Henry was not with that band. Sorry, Cap'n."

"Don't beat yourself up over it."

Night Runner looked his captain in the eyes, and their gaze exchanged apologies again. Still, it was not enough for Swayne. He had not been explicit.

"I'm sorry for going off like that."

"I gave you reason enough."

"We're not going into that again."

Night Runner's crooked smile showed his gratitude.

Swayne responded with a smile and a nod. With that, the incident was buried. Marines did not need to trade hugs and tears, to share heartfelt emotions in the light of day. Their relationships, more sacred than marriage vows in these times of combat, did not require the opening of veins or hearts.

With that, it was over. They both knew the topic would never come up between them again. The Marines might convene an inquiry, especially if they couldn't get Friel out of enemy hands. If so, they'd have to deal with it. But they would do so together. If that day never materialized, neither would the subject of Friel's kidnap.

Inside, Swayne tested himself. Did he really trust Night Runner? The answer was simple. Yes. How could you not trust the man to know what the warrior knew? He could identify his own soldier by a boot print as surely as the FBI could after DNA testing. In times of battle, Swayne needed the quickness and accuracy that Night Runner gave him. Quick decisions. Snap shots. Dead enemy soldiers.

If Night Runner had not killed the terrorist, the man whose arms were supposed to be tied behind his back with a rifle thrust between the elbows would have brought that rifle to bear on Greiner first, then Swayne. And the two terrorists behind him could have answered the Marines' fire with their own. This mission, already with its setbacks, serious as they were, would have ended in disaster. The loss of Friel was bad enough.

NIGHT RUNNER WAS glad that he could see the faith restored in him by the expression on the captain's face.

If the man only knew. If he had only experienced Night Runner's own fears. What if he had been wrong in his instant analysis of the boot prints? What if they had put Friel into their cloaks and sandals and made him trail the other two? Trading clothes happened often enough in hostage incidents. To foil snipers. What if—

He shook his head. It was wrong to doubt himself. He had already done that enough. He had beaten himself up over the loss of Friel. Time for regrets was over. He had paid the price. He had lived out the vision. The vision had been fulfilled. He had not killed his son, Friel.

In the end, he would bring back Friel to the fold.

In the end, Night Runner would prove to be right from the beginning. Friel would learn from this. He would be a better Marine for the experience, no matter how painful.

Although not a wrinkle moved out of position on Night Runner's stern, olive-complexioned face, he began smiling inside. In peace. In joy. He closed his eyes. Not to sleep. But to see into the vision again. To recall something he might have missed. Where was this to end, now that it had not yet ended after all?

• • •

THE BEAR HAD come in the blackest hour of night. Night Runner guessed the time to be not more than a couple hours before dawn. He'd spent most of the night on his feet, leaning back against the tree.

And most of the night he'd also spent questioning his own sanity. What kind of idiot smeared himself with bear bait and staked himself to a tree, waiting for a grizzly? How did that prove courage?

If the bear did not come, he was not brave but lucky. If the bear came and left because Night Runner started shouting, that did not make him brave. It just meant the bear was cowardly.

If the bear came at him and he fought back with the knife, did that mean he was a coward? Just for trying to save his own life?

If he threw the knife away, the medicine woman said, he'd be a coward. But if he kept it and didn't use it, he'd be a moron.

He had to die to prove himself a brave man?

These were the questions running through his head for the hundredth time when he heard the snapping of brush coming from downwind. He heard the snuffing and clacking of teeth.

The bear, a grizzly from the sound of it, was warning him. It was coming for the food it had scented. He'd better be gone when the bear arrived.

That was the warning anyhow.

Night Runner felt an instant of panic. He had time. Maybe not to run away, but he could cut himself free and climb a tree until the bear left him.

He'd never even have to face the woman again. He could leave, and she'd not say anything.

But she would know. Worse, so would he.

So he let the bear come to him. First, it stopped short of the first packet and sniffed hard. It bounced up and down on its forepaws, as if bluffing a charge. Then, overcome by the sweetness in the air, the bear scarfed up the fruit.

Once it had finished, it went to the nuts and seeds and lapped them off the foil. From there, it only took a second for the tongue to snake out of the huge jaws and lap up the fish parts.

To Night Runner, it felt as if he'd had hours instead of a minute or two to run things through his head.

He wondered. Did a man ever get a grip on bravery? Or was it just an automatic reaction? He knew of men who'd done reckless things in combat that had turned out well for them, even leading to decorations. Some men told of having no memory of acting bravely. Others thought, on reflection, that they'd just been dumb, overcome with panic at doing nothing, and so had done something rash.

He also knew of men who fought like dervishes one day and hid from danger the next.

In his culture, bravery was revered, and a warrior tested himself continually in non-battle situations. So when the day of fighting came, he would know how to handle fear.

Maybe that's all there was to bravery, he thought. Just a bit of conditioning.

Which left him here with a wonderful insight and a bear with a taste of fish scraps.

He could see well enough that the bear was a grizzly. He could smell the acrid scent of breath. He was certain the bear could smell the ooze of blood down his back.

The bear reared up. They faced each other, he the taller of the two, it the more powerful.

Night Runner held the knife still, his hand at his side.

The bear leaned toward him, sniffing. Then it let loose with a cough that morphed into a growl.

Night Runner flinched at the bad breath, but otherwise held his ground.

Only then did it come to him, the insight he'd been seeking. Bravery wasn't always a matter of skillful, courageous combat. Sometimes the bravest act was to keep the urge to strike in check.

"I understand, my brother."

SWAYNE HAD PUT his own mind in order. Night Runner had backtracked once each watch to check that nobody followed their tracks into the position. They all had inventoried their own ammunition, cleaned weapons, and packed for the night mission. Swayne had redistributed ammo from his supply, since he had fired his weapon the least. They were in good shape. They would have the day to rest and plan, the night to get into position to snatch Friel back.

Only one tiny detail nagged at him: *Snatch him back from where?*

As he waited for Winston to download electronic maps of the holy city and floor plans of likely hiding spots, Swayne reviewed the situation. CIA analysts would be checking the video record of the spy satellite downloads. Of course, once the terrorists got into the city, they would be more difficult to track. Except that they had entered two hours before sunrise, the time at which most of the population would be sleeping hardest.

Swayne had made it clear to the intel types that he did not necessarily need to have them waste their time on rehashing what had gone on during the night in thermal record. They could look that over after the mission. If they had suggestions, and if by extension Zavello had asschewings to hand out, there would be time enough for that later.

What he wanted to know was, where were the most likely hiding places? And once that was decided, could anybody provide floor plans?

The first piece of news was the best. Winston reported that Mashhad had been mapped in detail when the United States was still an ally of the Shah of Iran. The Army,

Navy, and Marine Corps had maintained listening posts right alongside the CIA during the Cold War. They had been stealing electronic emissions from the Soviet Union for decades. And even before instability had begun to shake the Shah's rule, the same intelligence types had had enough sense to photograph buildings inside and out and steal floor plans.

Many an Army sergeant had gone on holiday to even the smallest towns in the country to visit the natives and spend American money on trinkets. To photograph themselves in front of buildings and churches. And inside buildings and mosques. Markets. Public squares.

"The problem is not that we do not have information about these older buildings," Winston told Swayne over the radio. "The problem is that we have so much of it."

"We also got the rest of the day to sort it out," Zavello said, not so much a report as an order.

By nightfall, Swayne had slept as much as he intended. For that matter, as much as he could. His first nap had been a brief one, only as long as necessary to get over the effects of his fatigue. Once that had been taken care of, he stayed wide awake. His alarm clock was the lack of preparation for the evening's mission. He would not rest again until he had at least put together a preliminary plan.

That he did during his turn at the watch. From a position among the boulders, he could look out over the city. It seemed so large and sprawling. How could they ever penetrate it, remain invisible, and navigate to a terrorist stronghold to find a Friel in a haystack?

Those ideas he put out of his head. They were Marines. They would penetrate it. They would go directly to the spot identified as the most likely place to find Friel. They would move through the building like burglars. They would kill anybody who got in their way. They would either find Friel or they would move on to the second most likely place. Hell, if they had to take apart every root cellar in the city, they'd find Friel.

Once he had resolved that in his head, he waited for blueprints, photographs, and maps.

Zavello had told him he would keep an ear tuned to the highest intelligence circles, those that intercepted electronic traffic, pulling electronic signals from the skies and turning them into words.

So far, nothing had been transmitted. Whoever was down there on the ground was keeping tight-lipped.

Who knew? Maybe they did not want to turn over their prisoner to the religious fanatics among the Ayatollahs. Maybe their idea was to try to sneak the U.S. Marine out of Iran by night. Perhaps into Afghanistan.

With some tentative plans in place, Swayne had felt comfortable enough to sleep briefly again in the afternoon. He had done so, even with the radio receiver in his ear still turned on. There was no idle chitchat on his tactical radio. Just some routine reports. Even those Zavello kept to a minimum. If it did not have the possibility of an immediate effect on the Force Recon Team, he wanted everybody in the tactical operations center to stay off the tactical net. He understood the simple need of soldiers in the field to get a rest. Forty to fifty men and women in OMCC might each have a single tidbit to contribute in the course of a shift, meaning three shifts worth of tidbits to nibble at the field soldier's peace of mind and body. The leader in the field could be overwhelmed with minutiae. Zavello—bless his nasty disposition—wasn't going to let that happen.

Finally, an hour before dusk, Winston downloaded an intel estimate of the situation and an updated bio of Azzan.

Swayne went to work on it. He skimmed first, taking in a sense of the situation, the city, and his man. Then he began to focus on reading about the man in detail. The situation and the city were not as important as Azzan. Swayne needed to know his enemy, the things in his personality that accounted for the pattern of last night's action in battle. The thinking. The tendencies. The risks. The arrogance.

As the sun winked good-bye over the mountains to the west of the city, Swayne thought he knew the man who he believed had directed last night's operation.

To his credit, Azzan had demonstrated a genius for small-unit operation. He had combined the best of sound conventional military tactics with a terrorist's need to remain flexible in the field. His plan had worked. He had sent the Force Recon Team, with all its superior technology, off in the wrong direction.

It fit. Swayne saw that Azzan had been a student of the conventional American military mind. Plus he would have had access to plenty of secrets. Not that they were such high-level secrets at those military schools. But many of the staff officers attending would have had jobs before going there. Jobs in high places. Somebody quite easily could have attended the secret briefing on military surveillance techniques and spy satellites. He could easily have spilled his special insider scoop about the true accuracy of the global positioning systems. Bragged about things that he had seen inside the Pentagon while working at a desk for the two years prior to going to Command and General Staff College.

Azzan had money. He had spread plenty of it around while he was at the Command and General Staff College. He had thrown parties. The report on him said that he did not drink. But he was not so against drinking and partying that he would not buy the finest scotches, wines, imported beers, Cuban cigars, and other forms of entertainment, including women, for his fellow officers. Yes, Azzan would have pumped the Americans for information in every way. He was known to be a smart man, full of charisma. He was a con man. A con man who already was rich and did not seek more wealth, but information that gave him power.

Swayne scrolled to the bottom of the report to read the conclusions of the intel analyst who'd submitted this report. He found that Azzan had as much access to technology as the Force Recon team.

But Azzan didn't care about toys. Or money either. He had enough of both to entertain all the fraternity boys on the East Coast for all of their college careers. He didn't like to gamble in the casinos. He didn't keep women as far as anybody knew. Didn't keep men or boys as sexual toys. He was radical, but not wed to any radical ideology.

No, for Azzan the excitement in life was the game. He was a player in a contest with life-and-death stakes. His satisfaction came in killing others and then bragging about his ability to elude the best the West could throw at him, building on his legend by thumbing his nose at special-ops forces from all the major powers.

Which played right into the hands of the Western press, which enjoyed tweaking governments of all kinds at every level.

Swayne rubbed his temples. If he was right about Azzan, what did that tell him?

Azzan had humiliated a Force Recon Team by stealing one of its men. First thing, his ego was not hardwired to share credit. So he was not going to give up Friel to the Iranians. He was not going to let anybody else have a share of his glory.

Second thing, there'd be no glory without the glory-makers, the press. Whether Azzan intended to parade his man inside Iran or simply make a ransom demand, he needed publicity. For credibility, it had to be the Western press. Specifically, to make the biggest splash possible, the U.S. press.

Swayne radioed Zavello with his theories about narrow-

ing down the search areas inside Mashhad. After a few
obligatory insults about his ability as a profiler of international terrorists, the colonel granted his requests.

When Swayne signed off, he felt that he'd recovered
his confidence, that he was back in the game as a first-
stringer.

Last night he'd started out fighting a terrorist. He had
used all the tactics that had worked before in fighting conventional terrorists, if there were such thing. Now he
knew that he could only win against Azzan by beating
him first inside the man's head.

That made Swayne smile. First, that he knew more
about his man than his man would ever know about him.
Second, that he still felt he had the ability to beat the guy
at his own game.

Once the sun had gone down, and the fireball's glow
had disappeared, Swayne could not wait any longer. He
was eager to get inside the holy city. Certainly, to recover
Friel. But almost as important, to kick Azzan's ass. Or,
to be more accurate about it, to let Azzan outsmart himself.

They had chosen an approach through irrigated fields
and orchards. These would be occupied and tended by
day, but quiet at night, Swayne thought. He was right.
They reached the edge of the city and hunkered down,
keeping watch, not to rest, but to wait for the city to rest.

They could not move about while Iranians were down-
town smoking and joking. While they waited, he kept getting intelligence updates from satellite information and
electronic interceptions, primarily cell-phone messages.

The National Security Agency had been monitoring
telephone emissions inside Iran for decades. By now
they'd been able to decipher government transmissions,
and more importantly for Friel's longevity, they'd cata-
logued the signatures of the standard transmitters. They'd
know the voiceprints of government officials. Down to

the models and probably the serial numbers of their equipment.

It didn't take long for intelligence to pinpoint a new transmitter in the mix, a digital device with burst capability and an encrypted signal, an apparent prototype of a Japanese model that NSA hadn't seen outside of Asia. They didn't want to talk about it.

Which probably meant they hadn't deciphered the code, Zavello theorized.

Swayne didn't care about the code or the conversation or the hardware or even the identity of the party that had been contacted. All he needed was a location from which the phone had been used.

He got three locations. And the contacts. One of particular interest. Zavello told him that Nina Chase had been reluctant to talk to anybody in the Marine Corps about the content of her telephone conversations. Zavello had told her he simply wanted confirmation for the sake of a certain Marine officer's life, career—and sexual potency, he'd added—whether she had recently been given an assignment to cover a breaking story in northeastern Iran, yes or no.

After a stunned silence, she'd murmured, "How did you know?"

Zavello had hung up on her, he said. Then he signed off with Swayne, leaving him to shape a plan for a search of the city.

Swayne studied the J-2 on Azzan's band and the scenarios that the intel people had worked up as to possible locations.

The satellite had tracked the party of men from the desert into the city. The group of seven had entered Mashhad from the city's southeast quadrant on the main thoroughfare, the Holy Revolutionary Way of the Most Honored Imam Khomeini. The name brought a twitch of a smile to Swayne's lips. *Some road sign there.*

Swayne asked for the download of the raw satellite imagery. He tried to pick out details that would identify Friel, but the resolution of his handheld computer screen wasn't fine enough to tell one man from another. The group had traveled in a tight knot down the main streets and disappeared into a mosque. The first distinct phone call had been made from there, uplinking to a French military COMSAT stationed over the Caspian.

Swayne shut down the replay and went back to the INTSUM, the intelligence summary.

Later, some thermal images indicated men leaving the mosque through a rear door, crossing a courtyard to a dormitory for clerics. It was a school for the young Ayatollahs. Foot traffic back and forth indicated lots of activity. By itself, worship at night was not unusual. The school required trainees to worship around the clock, around the calendar. Hourly bands of worshipers moved from the dormitories to the mosque and back. On this night, however, the foot traffic had been at irregular times, not just at the top of the hour as was the custom, according to long-term reports going back years. Swayne shook his head. What a job that must be, analyzing the movement of school students month in and month out.

Again, the INTSUM reported, the satellite imagery was not clear enough to indicate whether Friel had been moved out of the mosque with the individual terrorists that had moved through. The analysts had made the mosque and the dormitory first and second choices of likely places for Friel to be held—a second digital phone call had been made from the dormitory. Very likely, the INTSUM reported, Azzan and his group would move Friel out during the day. They could get into traffic in the bustling street of Mashhad and disappear easily.

Other foot traffic had been seen leaving the religious compound, both walking and driving to an elegant residence a half mile away. The building had been an Army barracks during the reign of the Shahs, but had been converted to an officers compound for the new Revolutionary Army of Iran. One compound within the main compound had been known to be a strategic meeting center for terrorists sponsored by both the Ayatollahs and the military inside Iran. A third digital call had come from there.

Other pertinent traffic identified by the CIA included movement to and from a palace a mile away from the barracks, once a retreat for the Shah, built in the fifties to resemble the White House in Washington, D.C., and occupied by a royal cousin but never visited by the Shah himself. A fourth call had come from there.

Analysts used the digital phone to track the movements of Azzan, assuming he'd be the only man to use the high-tech phone. Swayne agreed. The man liked his toys. Even more, only he would be permitted to stay in touch with his corps of publicists, the American press.

The analysis went into great detail about the importance of deciphering the newest scramble codes that hadn't yielded to an all-out effort to break them. Swayne didn't care what Azzan was saying. He only needed to know where the phones had been used. So he could find Azzan. So he could kill him.

The INTSUM noted that military security had been stepped up outside the mosque and around the dormitory. Extra guards had gone on duty, more than double but less than triple the ordinary sentry disposition. The alert level at the barracks had been increased in the form of doubling the number of guards that normally walked their posts. And every building with a roof big enough to allow a helicopter to land at the barracks now showed sentries in place—normally, the guard bunkers on the roofs stayed empty.

According to the analysts, nothing in the security status had changed at the palace since the first flurry of activity. No military vehicles, no outposts, no guards.

The report suggested that the officers quarters was a third likely holding area for Friel, perhaps the best choice, since it would have cells, interrogation rooms, and torture chambers. Military officers would insist on being well guarded around the clock since they were part of the personal security forces for the Ayatollahs.

The analysts had recommended looking into the mosque first, the school second. The reasoning went that those places would be the least likely areas to be struck by an American military force, therefore the most likely places to hide an American prisoner. The officers compound at the barracks was a strong third choice.

From the tone of the reports, Swayne didn't believe anybody thought he was going to get into any of the sites. Let alone get Friel out.

So far, nobody had ordered Swayne into any of the areas, leaving the decision to the officer on the ground closest to the action. No way was intelligence going to take responsibility in case they were wrong. They were only too happy to let the man on the scene deal with the situation—and the flak that was sure to come afterward if the intelligence was wrong.

Zavello's gruff voice broke into Swayne's thoughts. Swayne knew from the tone that something was up, something that Zavello didn't like. Something that Swayne would not like either. Of that he was sure.

Swayne responded, "This is Spartan One."

"Spartan mission is canceled. You are to E & E and proceed to Pickup Point Echo. Spartan team is to be extracted. Do you copy?"

Swayne didn't answer. He was speechless. Here he was, at the gates of the city, and somebody had lost their nerve. Zavello? He'd doubted it.

"Spartan, acknowledge." Zavello's tone had hardened. He might not like what he was having to tell Swayne, but Swayne had better damn well answer.

"Request background."

Swayne was asking for an explanation, a rare thing. Marines did not demand that their bosses explain orders. Marines did what they were told and when. It was fine to ask, "How high?" But "Why?" No way.

Swayne had kept any tone of insubordination out of his voice. He was simply asking for clarification. He hoped it wouldn't bring the wrath of Zavello's brimstone.

Zavello explained in clipped sentences. "Spartans are to extract themselves. Now. LGBs in transit."

Swayne felt sick in his gut. Bombers had been launched, Zavello said. Very high-altitude bombers. All three targets were going to be hit with laser-guided demolitions. Swayne knew of these weapons, made of compounds that would leave the chemical signature of a truck bomb, diesel fuel and ammonium. Primitive devices like that set off in Oklahoma City. That would solve the problem and suggest to the world that a rebel group within Iran had struck at the Ayatollahs who ruled with all the finesse of a medieval inquisition. The munitions would get a few terrorists and take out evidence of an American embarrassment. All in one stroke. Another bombing in a Third World country. The accusations would fly. The world would shrug.

Now all that remained was for Swayne to get the hell out as well.

Swayne remembered an earlier mission. A bomber had been launched back then too. With explosives sent right down the chute transmitted by the team's electronic devices. Only quick thinking on Swayne's part had prevented the Spartans from being blown away.

He wondered.

In fact, he had to know. "Eagle One, this is Spartan One, request you advise me whether this strike is going to be similar to any other I have known."

There. He'd said it: *Colonel, are you going to send a bomb my way? Again?*

"Negative," Zavello said, coming back at once.

Swayne believed him. Zavello would have found a way to tip him off. The colonel was not going to be involved with murdering a Force Recon Team that still had the capability to escape. If the political leadership within the U.S. didn't have the same scruples, that was their problem. But Zavello was not going to do in Swayne.

Meanwhile, Swayne came up with several alternatives to just running away to a rally point. The best one gave him one slim chance to recover Friel.

"Request permission to provide laser guidance and BDA."

Zavello keyed his mike to reply, but did not answer right away this time. Swayne guessed the colonel was trying to outguess him, trying to decide whether he should aid and abet the ploy to get around orders. "Stand by."

Swayne didn't know what was going on, but he could hope. He could hope Zavello was getting on the horn to the White House. He could hope he'd tell them that the most accurate way to deliver those bombs with the least amount of collateral damage was to allow one of the Force Recon Marines on the ground team to direct the strike using laser beams that were standard on their weapons. What's more, he would say, appealing to the prurience of every politician, the Spartans could take video. The White House would then be able to see strike's effect almost immediately. *Why, Mr. President, the team could transmit the digital packages directly to satellite. Raw video footage, either in IR or ambient-light illumination, would be on hand to counter any press or propaganda reports about where the strikes hit and what damage was done.*

The politicians could not resist that, Swayne thought.

The idea was almost too seductive, he hoped.

Zavello came back twenty minutes later. "Spartan One, this is Eagle One."

Swayne knew. By the tone of his voice, the Spartans were in. Sure enough, Zavello gave him two locations from which to get to rooftops where he might be able to direct and assess strikes on all three targets at once.

Swayne responded, "Roger. Request ETA for the Pave Nail missions, over."

Zavello gave him the scheduled time for the strikes. Then the colonel hesitated. Swayne knew he wanted to caution him about deviating from the plan the colonel was giving implied consent to. But Zavello could not say a word without confessing to it and getting it called off.

"Eagle One, out," he growled.

Swayne called a council with his team and snipped his fingers like scissors in front of his mouth. Night Runner and Greiner shut off their microphones too. He gave the briefest of briefings.

"Get ready to move out," Swayne said. "I want to be in position before somebody in the White House gets cold feet and calls us back. Any questions?"

Nobody had anything to say, although Night Runner did raise one eyebrow and flick his head in the direction of the busy city.

"What?" said Swayne. "The traffic and activity?"

Night Runner nodded. "Six hours, Captain. That would be cutting it close even if we didn't have to worry about citizens sounding the alarm."

"It's risky, yes."

He did not have to list the risks. His men could see them for themselves. Hell, they did not even have to look. The sounds of raucous traffic in and around the city told them everything. The Iranians were like people in cities the world over, loud and obnoxious, laying on their horns, shouting at pedestrians, playing their radios too loud, squealing tires, roaring, jockeying, racing. The heart of

this town, holy or not, was not even going to begin set-
tling down for six hours. Moving from the fringes of the
city into the neighborhood of the mosque seemed impossible for three men carrying weapons and wearing helmets.

That was another thing Swayne decided to bitch about:
special-ops troops wearing helmets to carry the power
packs for so much electronics gear. That was a dumb idea.
If the techies couldn't find a way to shrink the technology—

What was he thinking? The team had to get out of this
situation alive before he could bitch about the scientists
and their toys.

Hell, if they did survive, he'd be too happy to start
griping.

Night Runner held up one finger. "Wait here." He
pulled out the pocket-sized calculator that concealed his
PERLOBE and handed it to Swayne. Swayne nodded.
They were to remain in place for five hours or so before
getting into position to direct the bombs. It would not do
for any of their electronic beacons to be detected dashing
around somebody's observation screen. After Night Runner vanished into the shadows, Swayne took off his own
PERLOBE. He looked to Greiner, who had already removed the dog tags that contained his. Swayne moved to
disperse the PERLOBEs in a way so the arrangement
would look like a Force Recon Marine team in a defensive
posture with a scout out.

Greiner pointed up into the air.

"You can talk," Swayne said.

"What about the satellites? Won't they spot Night Runner?"

"No," said Swayne. And it was not bravado. "Not the
way he moves around. Not unless they have an imager
that can look through foliage and see through rooftops."

•　•　•

NIGHT RUNNER USED his GPS to identify the relative position of the satellite overhead. He found that the one he was looking for, the one with thermal-imagery capability, had moved into the northeast quadrant of the heavens. So all he had to do was keep something between himself and that part of the sky until he was clear of the Force Recon area. Very likely, the satellite was not watching the team anyhow, now that its operators had been told to expect the Spartans to remain in place. They would be gathering other intelligence data. Most likely, they had zeroed in on the mosque, the school, and the officers barracks to maintain surveillance at high resolution, high magnification.

Of course, he would not assume that.

To be on the safe side, he kept in thermal shade until he was well clear of the area. Then he moved like any other thermal image—namely, the civilians moving around the city. Before long, the satellite could not pick him out of the crowds of thousands in the city.

ZAVELLO HAD TOLD his operators to pay no attention to the disposition of the PERLOBEs outside the holy city. He wanted Swayne to make his move without the chance of being detected. It hadn't taken him long to figure out what Swayne had been asking for in his request to remain in position and direct strikes. Hell, if Zavello were in the field, he would be doing the same thing. Since he wasn't on the ground, the least he could do was act like a magician's assistant and wave the cape with a flourish, directing the eyes of his audience away from the Swayne's sleight of hand. He began giving orders and snapping at the people on duty in the OMCC. Make them focus on him and not the possibility that a team in the field and the crazy colonel in charge of the operation were in the process of sidestepping orders from the President of the United States.

Of course, Zavello's rage was not all bluff and bravado.

If Swayne were to get caught with his pants down, Zavello would have to cut him loose, act innocent, testify against the best captain he'd ever worked with in the Marine Corps, watch him be convicted and go off to serve life plus twenty at Leavenworth.

Hell, he told himself. What was the worry? There wouldn't be enough of the poor dumb bastard to come home and stand court-martial anyhow. Those boys weren't going to get out of Iran alive.

No, he told himself, he wouldn't be so pessimistic. Swayne wasn't going to disobey any orders directly. At least not in a way that could disgrace the Corps. He was just an eager officer trying to get into position to direct bombs.

Without drawing attention to himself, Zavello asked for a periodic swath of the spy satellite's thermal camera to make a pass along the most likely route that Swayne and his group would have to take to get inside Mashhad.

"You make damned sure that no Iranian military unit stumbles onto that team," he said. That worked. Zavello tried to see when Swayne and his group left their hiding place. Once, he saw a figure move out of position into the open, as if taking a leak. Then the thermal-spot oval disappeared into the trees again.

Zavello did not see it again. Really, he didn't expect to. These were Force Recon Marines. They were supposed to be invisible to anybody, including spy satellites.

He found himself cheerleading for them. *They damned well better stay out of sight*, he thought. *Or I'll be waiting for them when they get out of Leavenworth so I can kill them myself.*

NIGHT RUNNER LED them the way that he had reconned. He took the team inside a culvert so they could cross the main highway without being seen by the enemy on the ground or the friendly eye in the sky. Then the Marines dropped into a storm drain. Clearly, it had been dry for months, and most likely could stay dry for years. When the storms did hit this part of the country, though, they would be ferocious. Flash floods would come from every direction. This Night Runner knew from his analysis of the area in the pre-mission briefing. Swayne might understand his enemy and strategies for getting at him. But Night Runner understood Mother Earth better than anybody in the Marine Corps.

Next, Night Runner turned and led the team against a low wall that was flanked by shrubbery. He picked up a juniperlike bush that he'd cut on his recon and demonstrated how the others should hold theirs. Swayne and Greiner found their own shrubs, and held them to break up the outline of a soldier dressed in a helmet.

They moved three steps at time, then froze for a second before moving another three steps. If they had walked at a normal pace, they would have been seen. But this movement technique made them seem like just three more junipers and shadows in the myriad of shadows flitting against the wall as traffic passed by, two hundred headlights a minute.

A mile farther along, Night Runner felt confident that they would not likely be picked up by the spy satellite overhead. So he became less concerned about shielding them from the sky, and more concerned about their next obstacle, a military checkpoint. All traffic had to stop at the gates to the city. When he had been by before, he had watched only two minutes, enough to pick up patterns and attitudes of the guards.

The traffic was heavy, and guard procedures were routine. Attitude was lax. Even if the Iranian security force had been told of the team's presence in the desert, nobody here really expected three Marines to try to drive into the city. An armed guard at the checkpoint always went to the rear of every cargo truck and checked inside every set of doors not padlocked. The guards also looked inside vans and the cabs of trucks. They flashed a beam into a few backseats of cars before waving the traffic through.

Clearly, the Iranian civilians weren't used to the delays. Many drivers honked. Some, once they'd passed by, gestured at the guards with the universal one-finger sign of disrespect.

So Night Runner concluded that some security had been stepped up at the checkpoint. Nobody was taking it too seriously, except for soldiers checking trucks. That made it seem fairly obvious to him that the team should not sneak through the checkpoint in a truck.

Finally, he reached the farthest point of his recon. With his eye, he followed the fence that stretched into the night on either side of the checkpoint. He knew from satellite images that the wire ran for miles both ways. Guards patrolled, either in pairs or with dogs. He turned to the captain and Greiner. The Marines turned their heads and leaned in close to hear above the rush and roar of traffic. "We can't pull anything Hollywood here," said Night Runner. "No trucks. No way to fight our way into the city."

"What do you recommend?" Swayne asked.

Night Runner shrugged. "I'll sneak under the wire, see what's beyond the checkpoint, and signal you."

"IR?"

Night Runner grimaced. "In Morse code."

"My Morse is rusty." Swayne turned to Greiner. "How's your Morse? Maybe between the two of us."

"Sir. Gunny." Greiner bit his lip.

"It's okay if you don't know the Morse code," said Swayne. He could hardly reprimand the man when he had just admitted to the same weakness. That was the thing about high-tech toys. They let the basics get rusty.

"I'm worried about the guards and dogs," said Night Runner. "If we leave any bodies, they'll know we're coming after Friel. He'll be moved, and we'll never find him."

"What's your Plan B?" said Swayne, who wasn't all that sure they'd find the kid from Boston anyhow. But before Night Runner could answer, Greiner spoke up.

"Sirs, I have a better idea."

Swayne's first reaction was to snap at him. But this was not the kind of smart-ass remark he was used to from Friel. Friel's idea would have been to attack the checkpoint and fight their way into the city, killing as many of the enemy as they could regardless of whether they could accomplish the mission. In other words, a waste of words.

Swayne looked to Night Runner. He didn't want to counter a plan that the gunny had suggested. But Night Runner was not too proud to listen. He shrugged at Swayne, and they looked to Greiner.

"What is it, son?" said Swayne.

"I've been watching the motorcycles. I used to ride motocross, so I always watch motorcycles when I see them. The guards at the checkpoint are checking some cars and vans at random. Most of the trucks too. But I noticed they're paying no attention to people going in on motorcycles. They don't even give them a look, just wave them by. They expect us to try to get in by truck. Or maybe to sneak in, which maybe we could do. Motorcycles they ain't expecting. We can do it."

Swayne looked to Night Runner. The warrior was already studying the traffic flow at the checkpoint. "He's right. And some of those people are dressed in their blankets too. Some are wearing towels over their faces. We could do it."

Swayne said, "You can ride? Any brand?"

Greiner smiled his best aw-shucks smile. "Everything. Anything."

"You've never mentioned motorcycles before."

The kid shrugged. "All I've ever wanted to be is a fighting Marine. I didn't want anybody to stick me into some kind of messenger service. Or military police. At first, when people asked me what my skills were, I would say motorcycles, and they would laugh at me. So I stopped saying it. But I can ride a bike, sir. I'm as good at riding as Gunny is at tracking, Friel is at shooting, and you are at thinking things out. Maybe I can't do any of those other things worth a damn. But I can ride a bike better'n anybody on this team."

Night Runner looked to Swayne for approval. Swayne shrugged. *Why not?* Night Runner did one of his disappearing acts.

IT FELT STRANGE to Night Runner to be doing work that somebody else had suggested besides himself or Swayne. But Greiner's idea was a good one right from the start, not only for getting past the checkpoint but for what would come next. They would not have to creep through the city. Put him in the woods or on the desert, and he felt perfectly at home. But in the city, even Stateside, he was out of place, and he knew it. Other people seemed to know it as well. People stared at him. People smiled, as if they knew he was lost, if not geographically, at least culturally. He would be only too glad to get a motorcycle for the kid to drive. They'd drive past the checkpoint and easily save an hour of sneaking and creeping to get to the place where Azzan was hiding Friel.

He found another culvert. It was a quick trip beneath the roadway and down the opposite ditch until he came to an intersection that fed into the main thoroughfare. During a break in traffic, he slipped across the roadway and into the opposite ditch. There he waited until he saw what he needed: a bike big enough to carry three Marines. With two riders. And not in Western dress, but both in burkas, long flowing robes, both women abiding by fundamentalist tradition, keeping their faces covered. Nothing was close behind them.

The women slowed at the yield sign, waiting for a break in traffic on the main thoroughfare. They both focused on the crush of cars and trucks, and did not see him as he stepped onto the roadway behind them to the left of the bike. One swing of the rifle struck them both alongside their heads, knocking them over. He caught the bike and shut off the engine by turning the key on the handlebars. He stepped on the stand and hauled the bike backward to keep it upright. Then he dragged both women into the ditch.

A set of headlights swept the bike above, and Night Runner clenched his teeth, hoping that he wouldn't lose his prize to another thief of the Iranian persuasion.

He heard a shout as the car stopped. He bit his lip, hoping that the car would ease into the traffic and be gone.

But no, a car door slammed shut.

A voice hollered from the car, and a second voice answered from the edge of the roadway.

Night Runner guessed at the conversation being carried on in Farsi:

Hey, looky what I found.

It probably broke down.

Let me check.

Hurry up before the cops come along and catch you, or the owner comes back and rips your head off.

The Iranian head came into view, all its attention focused on the bike. The body whirled, and Night Runner knew the man had flung one leg over the saddle.

He could let the Iranian steal the bike and make him wait for another. One of the women moaned. She was an innocent who had paid a price to help him complete his mission. The least he could do was make tomorrow's headache have a value for him, if not for her.

Night Runner took off his helmet and set his rifle aside. A moan from the second woman complicated his life even further.

Above, the man had turned the key and tried kick-starting the bike.

Hurry up, man.

Night Runner decided. He reached the top of the ditch and stepped onto the roadway just as the bike started up with a roar.

Well, would you looky here.

Look out behind you, man!

Night Runner could imagine how it looked to the driver of the car in the roadway. His buddy grinning wide as the motorcycle engine fired. A blur of motion, a woman's veil flying in the breeze, the figure of the tallest woman he'd ever seen coming into view to tower over the rider, who was now throwing his weight forward to rock the bike off its stand.

Night Runner began slapping at the thief, who howled in shock. The driver of the car howled too, in laughter. Both shrieked as Night Runner lifted the man off the bike and ran at the car, carrying the thief like a battering ram. He drove the head of the Iranian into the door with a crunch of bone and metal.

The laughing stopped, and Night Runner drew back the limp body and crammed it into the passenger seat.

The driver tore off, nearly causing a pileup on the highway. He forced his way into the stream of rushing cars and disappeared, the legs of the would-be thief still hanging into the night.

Night Runner was relieved the driver had turned away from the checkpoint. He turned the bike and walked it off the roadway. He felt certain the driver wouldn't report the incident, even if the thief's neck was broken.

He rolled the bike down to the bottom of the ditch, turned off the key, and laid it on its side. In moments, he had pulled the rest of the flowing garments and head wraps off the women. They were not so strict in their religion that they did not dabble on a patch of perfume, and the scent pleased him.

He was surprised at their undergarments, thong panties and skimpy bras. The women had definite tan lines. From bikinis. Perhaps they were Muslim women by night and cocktail waitresses at poolside by day. He didn't know, didn't care. He carried them into the culvert because their skin seemed so bright in the ditch, and he was afraid they'd be spotted by a passing motorist. He applied two strips of duct tape, the bad-ass variety, to keep their mouths shut for a long time. A handful of nylon zip-strips made shackles and hobbles to keep them immobilized. Then, carefully, so as not to run over them, he pushed the bike into the culvert, carrying the bundle of dark clothing under his arm.

As Night Runner led Swayne and Greiner into the culvert, Swayne was surprised several times over. First, that Night Runner had gotten the bike so quickly. Second, that two scantily dressed women lay sleeping peacefully on the concrete. Third, that he was about to dress up like a woman, a Muslim woman at that, and try to ride into the Mashhad with two other macho Marines. He felt as if he'd been hijacked into a Three Stooges film.

But the rest of the caper came off just as simply as Greiner's plan. Greiner drove the bike, sitting on the gas tank, draped in the robes from his wrists down to his ankles. Night Runner, smaller than Swayne, snugged up behind him, and Swayne draped Greiner's cloak over his back. Night Runner held two weapons close to his body. Swayne, his carbine stock telescoped down at his chest, slipped into the last robe, wrapped a head towel around his face, and sat on the last couple of inches of the saddle. He barely had a grip on the seat beneath Night Runner when Greiner manipulated the gears and the bike took off, sliding into traffic, weaving right and left around trucks and buses, as though Greiner was not only a good rider, but an Iranian rider.

They had left their helmets, NVGs, all their packs but one—which Greiner wore backward, making him look pregnant—and other excess gear, hiding it in the shrubbery.

As Greiner had observed, and Night Runner had confirmed, nobody even looked their way at the checkpoint. Except for one guard who whistled at them and made a gesture that had to be an obscene suggestion.

While Night Runner had been requisitioning the bike, Swayne and Greiner had worked out a system for navigating through the city. Swayne had memorized enough of the streets to get them going in the right direction. Like everything else so far, it was a simple plan. Greiner drove straight until Swayne put pressure with his chin on one of Night Runner's shoulders. Then Night Runner, whose hands were occupied holding weapons, would murmur under the garment to tell Greiner which way to turn. Only once did Swayne speak.

Night Runner said, "We're going to the mosque, right?"

And Swayne responded, "No."

In only ten minutes, Swayne pulled back on both of Night Runner's shoulders, and Night Runner said, "Pull over and stop." Greiner eased the bike up onto the sidewalk on a dark street, and turned into an alley between two three-story buildings.

"Helluva job, Greiner," Swayne said.

"Thank you, sir."

"Where are we? The barracks?" Night Runner asked. "I don't think I like traveling with my head under a lady's cloak."

Swayne and Greiner stripped off the burkas. Swayne said, "We are not going to the mosque. Not to the school, and not to the officer barracks."

Night Runner moved to the edge of the shadows so he

could look out on the street. His head came back as he looked upward at the building diagonally across the street, situated on high ground. "It's the palace," he said. "We're at the palace."

"Right," Swayne said.

Night Runner bit his lip. Eventually, a smile crept across his face, and the lip pulled out from between his teeth. "You're thinking that the bastard Azzan asked the Iranians to guard him and his American prisoner inside the mosque."

"Which the Iranians would be only too happy to do."

"So they would surround the joint with their own troops. Ditto the officer compound."

"But Azzan goes against the grain. Always pulling a scam. So far, he's gotten away with almost everything because his whole life is a history of bucking the conventional wisdom. Getting a line on him is as tough as nailing soft-boiled eggs to the wall."

"So he takes the most valuable prisoner he's ever had into the one joint where there is no security," Night Runner said.

Swayne nodded. "Now he thinks he's safe from us, and he's also keeping his American prize away from the clerics so they can't steal his glory."

Greiner looked back and forth between his noncom and his officer, his eyes dancing as if watching a tennis match. He kept his mouth shut. Like any Marine who did not want to be accused of thinking out of his pay grade.

Swayne checked his watch. Night Runner asked, "How are we doing on time?"

"Three hours until the strike. If we can recover Friel before then, we can call it off."

"But would we?"

Swayne shook his head. "Let's get the first part down first. Let's get Friel."

The toughest part of the approach was simply getting

across the street with all the traffic cruising up and down. They went one at a time, Night Runner first, so Swayne and Greiner could protect him.

GREINER RAN TOWARD the shadow where Night Runner had disappeared. His was an easy crossing, until he gained the other side. In the darkness, and without the night-vision goggles that they'd had to leave behind in the culvert, he was lost. He felt a hand on a shoulder, and Night Runner's soft voice said, "Stay put. Be ready to support the captain. You cover the downhill side of the street. I'll take the uphill."

Greiner was glad for Night Runner's ability to see in the dark, and his willingness to treat him like a fighting man equal to any other Marine. He hoped like hell that Night Runner wasn't going to get into any trouble over this business of losing Friel, which Greiner did not completely understand. The only thing that he knew was that something was wrong. And the three of them were trying to right it. He hoped that he could be a part of getting that job done. Much as he didn't like Friel, he knew that unless they recovered him, heads would roll. Most probably, Friel's first.

SWAYNE FELT THAT he had been touched by an angel when the traffic gave him a gap of at least a half mile in either direction behind Greiner. He darted toward the street and across the sidewalk. But before he had even gotten to the middle, he was caught in the headlights of a sports car that had slung itself around a corner just a block away and accelerated. He froze like a deer. If he ran across toward the others, they would all three be on the same side and would be less capable of doing anything. He turned and ran back between parked cars as the sports car, its engine revving high in a low gear, shot by. Then the brakes and tires grabbed the road. The car backed up abruptly. Swayne stood up and came face-to-face with a young Iranian, his hair oiled and his teeth shiny.

The man apparently saw nothing but a soldier. He called out to Swayne. Swayne guessed that he might be an officer with political connections. Or maybe a member of the government. Or more likely, one of the new class of wealthy Iranians that had sprung up to replace the vacuum of wealth after the Shah's family had been thrown out of the country, their wealth stolen in the purges that followed.

Swayne saw a recognition dawning on the man's face, and had already begun to raise his rifle. He cringed at the thought of a gunshot outside the palace where Azzan would be hiding.

But yet another guardian angel saved him. As the young man hit the accelerator of his sports car, his head fell off his shoulders into his lap as the sports car flew down the street, hit the curb, rolled, and landed on its top. Swayne followed Night Runner out of the street, quickly, as other traffic came downhill. They would find the wrecked car. And the driver. But not his head, which was rolling down the street next to the gutter, now disappearing underneath a truck near the street lamp.

Night Runner and his scimitar. Once again, the weapon had pulled them out of a jam. He was glad that it was in Night Runner's hands.

The rest of the approach went smoothly. Swayne and Greiner stayed in the shrubbery, blending into the shadows. Night Runner went ahead to scout for dogs and sentries. In a minute he came back to report there were none.

Before he let Night Runner lead them to the next spot, Swayne held up. He needed time to reflect, to get into the head of Azzan. Had the man pulled the sentries from around the palace? It made sense. His own men might be too tired to pull guard duty after a night in the desert. He would want to restore them before leaving the holy city, perhaps to get back to Afghanistan, where his havens were safer than here, where intrigue was the order of the day.

Swayne decided that Azzan would not have wanted any Iranian guards around. Even a squad of men would be granting the Army too much control. And as far as attracting attention to himself, what better way than to show that he was so unafraid of being discovered with anything to hide that he went to excess in the opposite direction?

Yes, that figured. He might relish the risk of not having guards around him.

Swayne shared his convictions with Night Runner.

NIGHT RUNNER MERELY pursed his lips and shrugged with his face.

"I don't know, Captain. It's out of my pay grade."

His job didn't include that kind of thinking. His job was to get them into the building and into the fight. No, he reminded himself, his job was to get Friel's ass out of this building and back home.

A commotion in the street behind them told the Spartans that passersby and neighborhood residents had discovered the gruesome traffic accident. Next would come some form of emergency response and an even larger crowd of the curious. Until somebody discovered the headless accident victim. A search would be launched for the head. There would be much hysteria when it was found. Maybe enough to keep this part of the city in disarray until the Spartans cleared the area.

It was a good thing for the Spartans to have such a distraction going on outside the palace. It might even draw some of the terrorists to gawk.

Swayne nibbled on the inside of his lip. If there were terrorists in the palace. So far he hadn't proved anything. So far all he had done was make some brash judgments about the thinking of his enemy, Azzan.

In the desert, the man had been able to outthink Swayne. Swayne himself had always been an advocate of changing his own patterns and routines to avoid being predictable. If Azzan was as smart as Swayne, he could expect something like that, sooner or later. The only advantage that Swayne and his team now had was that Azzan did not know that the Marines would be avoiding the mosque.

They crept up the slope toward the palace, keeping to the shadows, working their way through a garden of hedges and walkways made of crushed gravel. Night Runner kept to the grassy edges. Swayne thought he did so probably as much as to keep the gravel from hurting his feet through the soft soles of his moccasin boots as anything else.

No, he corrected himself. Night Runner would never sacrifice stealth to personal comfort. This was just stealth.

They reached a stretch of outbuildings alongside the palace, and stood leaning up against a gardener's shed to get their bearings. Swayne took in everything in one sweeping glance. Behind them, in the street, the crowd grew noisy, and small fights were breaking out among the gawkers, perhaps among people trying to loot the pockets of the victim or compartments of the car. So far, no ambulance. But sirens in the distance yelped their way through the streets. That situation had taken on a life of its own. So far, it had worked in favor of the Spartans.

He felt a hand on his shoulder. Night Runner pointed at one of the first-floor windows. Swayne saw what he had been looking for. Three men of the desert. They were dressed in clean robes, but they were rough men who had spent their days in the sun. He could see their toughness in their body language. They would be less comfortable bathed in the light of opulence, a crystal chandelier that backlit them, than lit by an oil lamp in a tent of skins.

Each of the three had an AK-47 slung over his shoulder. And crossed bandoliers of ammunition.

Swayne's face broke into a smile. For the first time since Friel had been picked off, virtually from under the team's nose, Swayne had a fix on the terrorists responsible. Azzan was in that building. With Friel.

Proof of that came when all three men suddenly looked over their left shoulders. Somebody was talking to them. No, somebody was yelling at them. Swayne could see them cringe. They pulled the curtains shut and the shadows disappeared from the window. Soon, the light went out.

Swayne put a knuckle to his forehead between the eyebrows and pressed hard, to focus on what might be going on inside the palace. He knew he had to assume the worst. What if Azzan wasn't buying the traffic accident? What if it seemed too coincidental to the terrorist? What if it meant the Americans had found their lair? That was the worst thing.

If so, Azzan's next move would be to pull out of the hiding place, perhaps get out of the city.

Was that a good thing or a bad thing? Should they burst inside and hit them on their own turf? Or should they wait until the band came out?

Good questions. The band might not come out at all. If Swayne was wrong in his assumptions, they could just as well be planning to stay here all night. In that case, the bombs would settle the issue by striking the mosque and barracks. If so, the terrorists would come out with rifles pointed in every direction, a pistol at Friel's head, afraid of an all-out assault. The answer was simple: The team had to go in.

He hissed in both directions, bringing Greiner and Night Runner to him. He opened the top of his computer, bringing up the screen that had the floor plan of the palace, downloaded by Winston. He oriented it for them, pointing to the shed where they now stood and toward the window where the three men had been gawking in the direction of the accident.

Swayne shared what he knew of the intelligence report more than twenty years old. No American had ever been in the basement of the palace beneath the ballroom on the north side, away from the street. An Army liaison officer to the Shah had left the ballroom once to use a bathroom and stumbled into a stairwell. He'd started down, but the Shah's guards had forced him away. Their clear lack of humor had indicated that the basement was a place clearly off-limits.

If Americans were denied entry into any of the Shah's facilities, there could only be one reason. People were tortured there. Perhaps kept as political prisoners. There might be bomb shelters, or secret escape passages too, but the one thing that seemed universal in Iran, before and after the royal family, was the never-ending need for torture chambers.

Swayne knew damned well the situation had changed. At least one American had been down there. His name was Friel.

Using his finger, he traced a path on the screen that Greiner was to take to get to the rear of the building. He gave Night Runner the opposite route, the long way around.

Swayne shut the computer and blinked twice, trying to get his eyes to adjust to the darkness after the illumination of the screen. A ghost of a figure remained in his eyes, so he blinked twice again.

But it was no ghost. And it had a pistol.

A pistol that went off, the bullet striking Swayne in the chest. He fell backward, cursing. His mission had ended. Likewise, his time in Force Recon. He had been hit hard. His air was gone. He could not inhale or exhale, and when he tried, nothing came.

Panic struck him. A sucking chest wound. He clutched

at his jacket and found the hole. He lay on his back, his finger plugging a wound in his sternum, fighting. Not for his country. Not to free Friel from the clutches of his enemy, not to kill a terrorist.

But for a single breath of air.

It did not come, and the blackness that covered his eyes was no longer from the night.

A shadow blocked the sky.

Swayne knew what came next. The finishing shot.

NIGHT RUNNER CURSED himself because he had not seen the man, had not heard a thing, did not smell him. He ran to the corner of the palace, no longer concerned about what might be inside. A shot had been fired outside. At his captain. A second one was about to come. He saw Greiner appear at the far corner of the building, leveling his rifle at the figure. Night Runner never skipped a step. He leapt and swung an arc with his right fist, the blade of his scimitar still streaked with the blood of the motorist.

The edge caught the man's shooting hand below the elbow and cut through both bones of the lower arm and into the chest, releasing the shooter's breath in a gasp. The man was trying to yell, but the musculature had been cut through, and simply pulled air into his lungs through the gash in his chest cavity instead of his throat.

"Stand watch," he said to Greiner.

"What about him?" Greiner said, gesturing at the fallen man's figure writhing on the ground.

"Forget him. He's dead, just not done twitching. Stand watch, dammit."

Night Runner, for the second time on this mission, felt a pang of fear that he had let down his team.

What had gone wrong with his senses?

Not that it mattered now. He bent over Swayne and used the blade of his knife to cut apart the captain's jacket. At least he was breathing. And the breath came in and

out of his throat. Night Runner saw he'd had the good
sense to plug the wound with his finger. That captain.
Always thinking.

He listened with an ear pressed to Swayne's bare chest.
The lungs were not gurgling. If the bullet had penetrated,
he'd be drowning in his own blood. And the heart. The
beat was fast, but regular. He did not hear squirting
sounds.

Holding the finger inside the wound, he rolled Swayne
on his side and felt all over his back and sides. That was
good. Nothing. No exit wound to deal with. He rolled
Swayne over to his back again.

Without removing the finger, he examined a chest
scarred with welts and wounds earned on previous Force
Recon missions.

Around the finger, he saw slivers of green composition
material with wires and circuits. On the ground beside
him, Swayne's computer had been shattered, shot through
from front to back the long way. The bullet had eighty-
sixed the battery packet for his radio as well.

Night Runner could not tell how much damage had
been done inside Swayne's chest, but it seemed possible
he might survive.

Provided Night Runner acted quickly to apply first aid.
And deal with the issue of people inside the palace, who
would be reacting to the gunshot by adding more firepower to the night.

He worked quickly. With a dressing, he dried Swayne's
chest around the wound, and pulled free as many slivers
and wires as he could clear without allowing air into the
chest, air that would collapse his captain's lungs. Then,
using some of Friel's bad-ass duct tape, he put a length
onto the skin and curled it toward the hole. In one sweeping motion he pulled Swayne's finger from the wound and
covered the entry hole. The tape sucked backward into a
concave divot. Swayne's chest was once again airtight.

Night Runner called to Greiner. Together, they bent over their captain.

"We're going inside. They know we're coming by now. If the traffic accident wasn't enough, that one over there has tipped them off."

"He's a gardener," said Greiner, as if that information would be helpful.

Night Runner shook his head. He could see the man's hand, scarred and gnarled, lying apart from his corpse, the severed fist still gripping a .45-caliber revolver as old as the OK Corral.

Swayne snorted, and Night Runner saw a grim smile.

He hoped Swayne did not get a look at the man. The idea of being killed by a veteran of World War II would probably send him into shock.

Night Runner's mind began to work at double speed. It had taken him a long time to adjust to being the gunnery sergeant for this outfit. Now he had to act in the capacity of officer as well. He had to do the thinking for the team, and decide how to execute this mission rather than just executing the job that Swayne gave him to do.

Before the computer had been blown to bits, he had planted the images inside his head. Now, the only thing to do was to make a direct assault on the building. Probably going through a window was safest, he told Greiner. The kid's eyes were wide, catching the lights of the city over Night Runner's shoulder. Helluva first mission, Night Runner thought.

"Let's go," he said. But they did not go. For Swayne's bloody hands held each of them by a shoulder.

"Captain," Greiner said in relief.

"Quiet," Night Runner said. "Let him talk."

Swayne managed to murmur to them both. Night Runner did as he was told, putting a concussion grenade in one of Swayne's hands, his carbine in the other. He did not arm the boomer, as Swayne had ordered. He did not want his captain passing out and dropping the grenade, blowing himself apart by accident.

He told Swayne as much. "We're going to take you out of here in one piece. With Friel."

Swayne pulled him close and whispered in his ear again.

Night Runner stood up, a look of relief on his face. Swayne had given him a plan. It seemed that half his problems were over, although any rational man would assume that they were only beginning.

SWAYNE'S JAWS KNOTTED, but not a sound escaped his lips as his two man dragged him into a clump of manicured bushes surrounding a fragrant tree.

Swayne, his rifle across his lap and his boomer at the ready, knew he was in for the fight of his life. Not necessarily that the terrorists would find him. Not necessarily because he might have to spend the night here and take them on during the day. No, his fight was going to be for one breath after another, until his team got him out of here.

NIGHT RUNNER AND Greiner ran at the building, no longer concerned with stealth. The sooner they got clear of Swayne's position, the sooner they could give him a margin of safety.

Running next to the palace, between the hedges and the quarry stone of the building, Night Runner went to the third large window from the corner. The lights were out inside. So he decided to take a chance. He punched his rifle butt through the glass and forced Greiner's head down. Nobody shot at them. So he punched out another windowpane and jabbed his rifle against the curtain. Again, he ducked. Again, nothing. He reached inside, threw two latches, shoved up the window, and again thrust against the curtain before ducking down. Again, nothing.

With that, he rolled over the windowsill and into the room. He went left. Behind him, Greiner's body crashed to the floor, screeching glass fragments against the marble as he crawled to the right. In seconds, they'd both looked around the corners of the curtains at each other. Nothing yet.

They bounded up and ran across the room toward the door that Swayne's computer had indicated led to the basement. The basement. That was all they knew. Whether the door was alarmed or guarded or barricaded or welded or had been covered over, they did not know.

They were simply taking the chance that this was the way to engage Azzan's men and their best chance of saving Friel.

They were in for a fight. Night Runner knew that.

He remembered Swayne's last admonition. "If you get contact, don't stay and fight it out," he'd gasped. "Pull back."

It took a while for Swayne's intention to sink in. But Night Runner, as he reached the opposite side of the ballroom, understood.

Azzan's men had been successful in the desert by leaving a delaying force behind and getting away with Friel. They had done it twice. Azzan would do it again, not because he was inflexible, but because it had been successful.

They were into the stairwell. Night Runner went down first. Soundlessly, for his soft-composition boot soles made no noise. They did not slap at the tiled steps like hard boot heels. They did not squeal like ordinary gym shoes. He walked as softly as if on carpet. As he reached the first landing, he signaled to Greiner without looking up. Three levels down, the two Marines found a hallway door.

Night Runner detached a cabled device from his rifle and looked into the sight. He put the end of the cable, a fiber-optic lens, under the door. To the right were three, no, four men. They were throwing furniture out of a room, building a barricade across the hall.

They were, in fact, doing exactly what Swayne had said they would do. Night Runner put his hand on the doorknob. Then pulled back. Once again, he manipulated his lens. He looked upward along with it to make sure no charges had been planted, to see whether any wires or alarms had been connected. He saw none.

So he slung his rifle and pulled a concussion grenade. He set the timer on the boomer, slammed the two halves of the round grenade shut, arming it. Holding a finger on the release button, he yanked open the door and rolled the device down the hallway toward the barricade. He slammed the door before automatic rifle fire filled the hallway. Then he waved to Greiner as he ran up the stairs.

"Let's go, Marine. *Let's go, let's go, go, go, go.*"

Night Runner simply did not want to be in a confined space when that grenade went off, multiplying its concussive powers, probably blowing the doorway into the stairwell. For that matter, probably blowing off the doorway to the ballroom as well.

They dashed into the huge ballroom, and Night Runner sensed the danger immediately.

"Hit the deck," he hollered even before Greiner came into the room. For himself, he held the door open, and was glad to see his man come sliding across the marble on his belly. Gunfire stitched across the doorway. Night Runner, who had been counting inside his head, slammed the door shut. No sooner had the latch hit home than an explosion from below rose up and stung his knees with the impact. The door blew off and flew across the room, striking a man standing there, the man who had held down the trigger of his AK-47. The combination of Greiner's bullets and the door striking him in the chest blew him across the room, through the curtains, and out the window. From outside, another man began shooting at the figure who had been blown out the window.

Night Runner's mind was busy. First, calculating that the gunfire from outside did not come from where they had left Swayne. No, those shots came from the lower lawn, perhaps by some statuary. Two rifles.

He signaled to Greiner to follow him. Hugging the wall, he moved toward the back of the palace, where huge French doors, three sets of them, showed what was going on outside.

But that was not a concern. A tiny squeal, a boot heel stepping on a fragment of glass was his concern. It came from behind an alcove. He remembered the position on the blueprint on Swayne's screen. A Persian rug hung over it. Night Runner dropped to his knees. Greiner followed suit. A man in flowing robes threw aside the rug and stepped into the room, his gun strobing, making him seem to be moving in stop-action. Bullets snapped over the heads of the two Marines. Night Runner cut off the man at the knees. Literally. One angry swipe of his sword passed through the lower thigh of both legs. For an instant, the blade had no effect. Then the two legs broke apart, and the man, now screaming, now no longer concerned about his rifle, landed upright on two stumps.

As Night Runner slashed again, cutting through the man's right arm above the shoulder and into the chest. Another quick blow across the neck and down into the cavity of the chest severed a quarter of the man's body.

Night Runner was up and running toward the back door. Because the captain had been right about everything so far, Night Runner knew what he would likely see outside.

He had made a count in his head. Four men downstairs as a delaying force. One man in the ballroom. Another from behind the Persian rug. That left four, perhaps five, from the original band in the desert. Two of those had been outside on the lawn. He had no way of knowing—

Two rifle shots. He recognized the sound. And the American gun, one of their own. Swayne's.

He listened for a few seconds, his heart unwilling to beat until he knew whether one of the Iranians had taken the rifle and shot the captain where he lay.

Two more shots. Deliberate and sure. That was a signature of the captain's firing. Other shots answered his. AK-47's.

Night Runner gave his heart permission to resume beating. He breathed in relief.

The captain had guts. He wasn't going to be able to shift into any alternate positions from where he lay. Not without the risk of puncturing a lung or one of the vital arteries in his chest. He was taking on the enemy anyhow, occupying one or two terrorists so Night Runner and Greiner could operate without being attacked from the rear.

One more shot from Swayne's carbine was followed by a shout of pain. Another shot. Another shriek.

There were no more reports from return fire. Night Runner amended his count. Two, maybe three of the terrorists were left. Including Azzan.

He reached the French doors and kicked one set. Then he dove out and left. Greiner dove right. The window glass shattered inward as an automatic rifle from outside opened up. Night Runner was up on one knee. The shooter was good. He did not fire over their heads, as the others had done. He was shooting low, about two feet off the ground. If he kept walking the rounds across the back lawn, he would be hitting Greiner's head any second. But no, Greiner flattened on the patio and rolled behind an urn.

Night Runner lifted his own rifle for the first time, using two quick bullets. He fired over the muzzle flash, putting one round on either side. The automatic fire continued. But now the bullets were rising up, taking out the beveled glass of the French doors. Then stitching up the side of the building. Then the upstairs windows, as the man fell over backward, his dead hand clutching the trigger until the gun emptied. Night Runner had never actually seen the man.

That left no more than two. Azzan and one other.

And Friel.

Meaning that the next time he saw one of his enemy, Friel would be in the bunch. He cautioned Greiner, "Don't shoot at any one of them unless you can ID the target, unless you're positive Friel is not in the line of fire."

Considering that he had just head-shot a man without ever seeing his head, that was good advice to be taking himself.

Night Runner heard the sound of an engine starting around the corner of the building. He saw the driveway, then the sweep of headlights. A panel truck, a cross between a station wagon and a pickup, came into view, careening down toward the street behind the palace.

Night Runner remembered that it was a service entrance that led into an industrial area. He saw that the gate was opened, that there would not be a clear shot at the driver unless the truck turned left, exposing the man's head. It did not. The vehicle flashed to the right and vanished behind the cultivated forest of trees and shrubs on the palace grounds.

Even as Night Runner was to his feet and running back toward Swayne's position, Greiner was on the move as well. Night Runner was beginning to like this kid. A lot.

As the kid fired up the motorcycle and pulled alongside Swayne's hiding place, Night Runner bent over the captain.

"Are you going to be all right for a minute?"

Swayne nodded. "Waste of time to chase him. Don't follow the truck."

Night Runner grunted, his tone a question.

Swayne spoke in quick snatches of words, his breathing growing more labored. "Head toward the officer quarters. Azzan won't run away. He'll be taking Friel to the garrison. He has to keep Friel. Or else he can't do any damage. To the United States."

Night Runner understood at once.

"Give me Greiner's radio," said Swayne.

Night Runner took a minute to peel the harness from Greiner and tuck it safely into Swayne's armpit. As he did, he kept checking his captain's face. He put a finger to Swayne's neck.

Swayne peeled the finger away. "I'm fine."

They both checked their watches at once. Both saw that they were within thirty minutes of the bomb strike. Unless they could pick Friel off in that time and send the planes away, the LGBs were going to fly.

"Get going," said Swayne.

He turned on the radio receiver. The tiny voice told him what he suspected. Zavello was missing him. And Zavello was pissed. Swayne did not bother putting it into his ear. He didn't want to hear it. Not now. Not when he had no intention of answering the colonel.

Swayne knew there'd be hell to pay once he returned to the States. He knew he deserved it too. First, he had not given a full report about the loss of Friel. Sooner or later, somebody was going to ask questions. Swayne was going to be forced into a position of telling the most awful truth yet about his team. Or lying. Which he would not do. Then this business of disobedience to orders. Zavello might understand because he had been a field officer, because he understood things like loyalty, which meant nothing to politicians—and for that matter, the military officers who had become more politicized than ever.

Even if Zavello put his own career on the line, he could not save Swayne from what was about to happen once he returned.

Oh, what the hell. The odds didn't look so good any-how. He put his hand over the spot on the bad-ass duct tape. The place where the bubble rose and fell with every one of his painful breaths. A flimsy hunk of tape. It was the only thing keeping him alive right now.

Rather than a sharp pain, a dull ache had spread across his entire chest. He could only breathe in short breaths.

There wasn't going to be any running across the desert for him. No climbing, no crawling, no nothing. He began to think of ways he could order his men to leave him behind. Nothing seemed quite strong enough. No matter what he said, they weren't going to abandon him.

He shook his head. He ought not to let the pain in his chest wreck the process of his mind. He should be trying to figure out the mind of his adversary.

What was Azzan up to?

No sooner had he asked the question than he saw a figure glide across the ballroom, lit only by the floodlights at the rear of the palace coming into the room through the huge glass doors.

He watched to be sure that nobody else would join that figure, perhaps one of the building's staff.

But then an enormous chandelier lit up the tapestry on the walls and the paintings and the statuary inside the room.

And Swayne saw that once again he had been out-smarted.

For there was Azzan, calmly pushing a cart toward the window as the sound of the motorcycle faded into the racket of the city.

Swayne picked up his rifle. He had a clear shot. Just as he'd been able to take on the two backlit figures that had fired into the ballroom a half hour go.

He checked his watch again. The bombers were due in less than twenty-five minutes now.

Where was Friel? Was he still in the palace?

It wasn't going to matter. He sighted through his night-vision scope, moving the invisible IR laser spot around the room. Azzan did not show himself again. He had simply moved the cart to the open window, the one that had been shot out, the place where the man had come through inside the curtain, worrying Swayne at first that it had been one of his own men.

He focused the rifle on the cart. It looked like an old series radio, something out of Vietnam or Korea.

Why would somebody with Azzan's resources use a radio like that, when he could communicate with something handheld that high-tech superstores sold around the world?

Swayne wished he could call Night Runner back. But they'd left all but one of their radios in a heap on the ground before climbing into the saddle of the motorcycle. Besides, he couldn't be sure that Azzan had kept Friel here.

He kept his rifle at the window. He still had some choices, even if Azzan had outfoxed him yet again. If the terrorist showed his face, Swayne would take him out. If not, he could blitz the radio. But what was the radio for?

NIGHT RUNNER CLUNG to Greiner's waist, the women's robes wrapped around his face again, hoping that Swayne was going to be right one more time, that his chest wound had not affected his thinking.

The smell of women's perfume on these clothes reminded him that he had left two noncombatants lying within range of his boomers, set to explode if anybody disturbed the night-vision goggles, helmets, and other gear left in the pile near the culvert. He had tried to keep the women clear of the concussion. Even if the grenades didn't harm them, they might die of humiliation at being found naked by Muslim extremists. The tan lines alone would convict them. Clearly, they had been outdoors in skimpy clothing, perhaps at the officers compounds, where Greiner was now headed, directed by pressure on his waist to turn either right or left as the intersections came up and flew by.

Night Runner dismissed the women. They were just two more instances of things going wrong on this mission. Or, to be accurate about it, things that he had caused to go wrong.

Now he wondered whether this team was going to get out of Iran alive. Or even dead. Friel had been driven off in a van. Swayne lay wounded beneath a tree beside an enemy stronghold. It was just a matter of time until emergency forces or military troops stormed the palace grounds looking for the source of that gunfire.

The two of them were chasing across the city without really knowing for sure whether Swayne had been right about—

The van.

It streaked across the intersection in front of the motorcycle. Even before Night Runner pushed against Greiner's side, the kid had leaned into a right turn. Night Runner saw the right wrist crank downward, the left twitch, as the motorcycle grabbed another gear and hugged the road tighter, accelerating to 125 kilometers an hour, about sixty miles an hour. The kid could drive a cycle, just as he had said. He shifted so cleanly, Night Runner at first thought the machine had some kind of automatic transmission. But no, his feet and hands worked as if they were part of the cycle.

They were gaining on the van as it sped toward the mosque and not the barracks. Swayne had been wrong about the enemy's intention? How many more things could go wrong on this damned mission? Friel snatched. Swayne shot. The team split up. What more?

Night Runner put his mind to work on how they were going to stop the train wreck of this event scenario. Start-

ing with the van that Greiner was preparing to pass. What
were they going to do? Pull alongside and assassinate the
driver? Hope it didn't crash and kill Friel?

At the thought of that outcome, he pulled back on Greiner's waist to slow him down. The van began to pull away
again.

Maybe they could wait for the vehicle to stop at an
intersection?

No, that wasn't going to happen. This driver was in a
rush to get to the safety of those troops surrounding the
mosque.

But why was he racing toward the mosque? By now
he must have known that he had not been followed. What
was the urgency?

Night Runner glanced at the speedometer again. Greiner was pressing ninety miles an hour to keep from letting
the gap to the van grow.

The night air, filled with smells of exhaust and cooking,
suddenly began to sting Night Runner's nostrils. He knew
the acrid fragrance. Had they passed a factory? Careful
not to upset the speeding bike, he glanced over his shoulders. No, they were in a residential district.

He tested the air again, although that was not so easy,
as it was being forced up his nostrils—he glanced at the
speedometer, now at ninety-five miles an hour.

The smells were coming from the van. Kerosene. Ammonium.

They were barely three blocks from the mosque when
the van ahead of them hit its brakes and began swerving.
It was going too fast to make the turn into the compound.

Ahead, he saw things unfold.

Rank after rank of soldiers had begun pouring into the
street. No doubt they'd heard of the gunfight at the palace
and had been put on full alert.

The soldiers formed a wall at first, to force the van to
a stop. But soon the wall crumbled and men began run-

ning away as the vehicle hurtled toward them.

Night Runner shook his head. Easily fifty soldiers were in the street at that entrance alone.

Who knows how many might be covering the other gates to the grounds. There might be an entire brigade of Iranians around the mosque. Every one of those soldiers had his attention on the smoking, screeching tires of the van. They might know the vehicle. They might understand because they had been warned that it was coming. They might have expected it to be traveling fast, but certainly not as fast as it was now going.

"Slow down," Night Runner said. His voice was flat. They were not going to get to Friel in time. "Forget the van. We have to turn around and get back to the palace."

Greiner hesitated. "Gunny?"

"Stop," he said. "It's too late to find out if Friel is in the van."

Night Runner saw the vehicle skidding sideways, blue smoke boiling from the tires.

A swarm of soldiers closed in on the vehicle. And if he was not mistaken, he saw the sparkle of at least one muzzle blast.

A second later, he heard the crackle of many guns.

The soldiers had not expected the van. They didn't appreciate its threatening approach. For all they knew, three American Marines were in it, trying to rescue the man in the mosque—for the first time, Night Runner allowed that Friel could not be saved.

He murmured a curse word to himself. "Back to the palace," he ordered.

Getting back to Swayne was now the mission.

Face it, whether Friel had been in the van, the palace, or the mosque, the outcome was the same. He was lost. The best Night Runner could hope for now was to save Swayne's life.

•   •   •   •

FINALLY, SWAYNE UNDERSTOOD the answer to the puzzle.

His mind had been at it the whole time, looking so hard for a solution he'd almost forgotten about his pain. Forgotten about the thin layer of synthetic material that was keeping him alive.

That was no radio in the window of the palace. At least not a transmitter. It was a receiver. The dome on top, about the size of the teacup, was a satellite receiver. In the package on the cart, a plastic box about the size of a computer monitor, was enough electronics, probably worth a million dollars, to track United States satellites.

And aircraft. Perhaps even Stealth aircraft, which were on the way. Somehow, Azzan had enough intelligence resources—and certainly enough intelligence, personal mental intellectual type of intelligence—to determine that the Americans would be desperate enough even to kill one of their own, perhaps risking global embarrassment that could be denied. They could deny the bombing. That might be any terrorist. But they could not deny a captive American special-operations soldier.

So, Swayne realized, Azzan had set up the stronghold around the mosque. He had promised to deliver the American there to the Iranians.

The Iranian military deployment had tipped off the Americans, including Swayne. But Swayne, having figured differently from the CIA, had guessed that Azzan would be at the palace.

So far, so good. But what was his point?

Swayne raised his rifle at the shadow sliding across the room. His finger caressed the trigger. The laser spot picked up the profile of a man's head, the close-cropped hair tousled.

THAT THERE WAS no turban saved Friel's life.

Azzan had pushed the kid, tied to an ordinary office

chair with rollers, up to the cart where he'd left the radio receiver.

Azzan had not exposed himself. Swayne saw only his shadow leaving the room.

Swayne struggled to sit up. If he could make his way across the lawn, he might get to the window. If he could prop himself against the windowsill, he could stay there and signal to Friel. When Azzan showed himself again, Swayne could—

A pair of headlights flashed across the backyard.

A limousine began coming into view, ten feet at a time. The car swept down the driveway out of sight. Swayne rolled over and got to his knees. If he could stand up, he might get a shot.

But he could not stand up. He could not even remain on his hands and knees. The pain was not necessarily unbearable by itself. But somehow, it swept across his chest in both directions, radiating from the bullet hole at the center of his sternum. It shut down his shoulder muscles, and Swayne began to topple. With his last bit of energy, he rolled, so he would land on his back. So he would not puncture the tape across his chest. So he would not land on his side and perhaps force one of the fragments of his radio through the flimsy tape.

He tried to speak into his radio, to contact Night Runner, but he did not have even enough breath for that.

The clouds, black and fuzzy, began edging into his tunnel of vision. Swayne realized he was blacking out once again. And once again, he could do nothing about it.

He would awaken later, perhaps bleeding internally, perhaps dying. While Azzan, probably drinking champagne and cavorting with women, headed out of the holy city. He would probably go to the airport. Probably get on a jet, his private transportation. He would live. He would make other Americans die, many Americans. Including Swayne.

Than, all went black.

• • •

As Night Runner approached the palace, he could see crowds forming at the gates. Nobody dared go into the grounds yet. Night Runner understood. People had died trying to sneak onto that property before. Nobody here was eager to die now. Even so, the emergency crews would have radios. They would be calling the military. Soon the place would be swarming with police. Or soldiers. Or both.

Night Runner told Greiner to slow down. He pulled a boomer from his jacket underneath the flowing garments, armed it, and closed the two halves together. He tossed it into the street, and watched it roll downhill.

Once again, he hoped that no innocents would be killed. But if that was what it took—

He would have a lot to atone for. All his mistakes. Those two women at the culvert.

The driver of the sports car.

People standing in the street when that boomer went off.

His voice trembled as he tried to speak. He got a grip. Told Greiner to drive around to the rear entrance.

Greiner realized they had two choices. They could go inside the back gate and drop the bike, covering the hundred yards to the palace on foot. Or they could bust through and across the grass on the fly, hoping to avoid ambush by surprising the enemy. When Night Runner did not tell him to stop, Greiner gunned the motor right. It was an easy ride for him. The headlights were on; he had been in night motocross before.

Keeping to the shadows, traveling behind the foliage, darting first right, then left, he made it to the gardener's shed and growled inside.

Even before he shut down the motorcycle, Night Runner was off and out the door. But at least he took time to pat Greiner on the back. Greiner felt his chest expanding.

As if he would burst with pride. He had made it. Nothing could be more of a reward to him than that pat on the back from one of the best Marines he had ever met.

Now if only the captain—the best officer he had ever met—was still alive. He stood at the entrance of the shed, hiding in the shadows, looking for a target in his rifle. But apparently, the grounds were empty. As if their enemy had abandoned the place.

Below them, the concussion grenade went off. The flash-bang wiped out his nightscope for a second. In that flash, he saw a figure sitting in the window at some kind of computer screen or something.

He lifted his rifle. Nobody was going to get his men from behind. One burst would finish this. The only thing that kept him from firing was the caution that had been instilled in him by the example of Night Runner and Swayne.

And Swayne had told him (or was it Night Runner?) not to fire unless he could identify the target.

The laser beam came back from the wash of the burst first. He put it directly onto the head of the person sitting there. Still, he would not press the trigger.

Then his own sense of caution kept him from shooting. The person was not even moving.

Finally, the screen came back to him, and he saw that it was Friel sitting at that radio.

Although he did not have a radio set of his own, he called into the darkness outside the shed, giving a report to Night Runner.

Night Runner gave him instructions.

Greiner was off. What a double dose of satisfaction he was going to get from this night. He was going to be able to save Friel's butt. From now on, Friel could not give him any more static. Not only would Greiner be a combat veteran, but he would also save the man's life.

* * *

NIGHT RUNNER KNEW that Swayne had regained consciousness. Although he didn't open his eyes, the captain whispered a question, his throat raspy.

Night Runner leaned in closer. "What did you say?"

"How much time?"

Night Runner looked at his watch. "About two minutes." Where had the time gone?

"The airport."

Airport? "What about the airport?"

"The airport," Swayne repeated. "It's to the northwest." His breathing was labored.

"Save your strength."

Swayne snorted and grasped Night Runner's shirt. "Azzan. He's going to the northwest. To the airport, dammit. Can you redirect?"

"If there's time."

"Go."

Night Runner knew the floor plan as well as Swayne. He grabbed his rifle and ran toward the palace, hurtled into the window, past Friel sitting in a chair, and came up running.

It seemed an odd sight. Friel. Naked. Sitting in his chair beside some kind of contraption. As Night Runner went by, he saw the surprise in his man's eyes. The pain, the surprise, the fatigue, and, yes, the hatred as he recognized the sergeant who had caused all his pain and misery.

Night Runner did not have time to stop, did not waste time to apologize, even with a glance. He was across the ballroom and into the stairwell. He jumped over the debris of furniture that had been blown around the room. He knew from the floor plans that this stairwell went to a guard tower on top of the building. It was the highest point.

He ran so fast his heart barely had time to catch up with his effort. When he reached the top, he gasped for breath. Six floors up, he could look out over Mashhad.

On one side of the buildings around him he could see the glow of a huge fire. The mosque. But that was in the opposite direction from where Swayne wanted him. Instead he looked out to the northeast, searching frantically.

The airport. He saw it through his rifle scope, and recognized a part of the apron where three airliners were parked, one of them unmarked. That would be Azzan's.

Now there was the problem of directing the LGBs. They would be dropped from eight miles above. They would be preprogrammed, but they could be captured in flight after they were released.

Night Runner pulled his computer from his jacket pocket. Using an adapter wire, he connected it to his rifle sight and loaded the preprogrammed frequency given to the Force Recon Team before they'd entered the city, the frequency they were to have used to direct bombs into the barracks and the religious quarters in the mosque compound.

As the bombs flew toward the target, somebody with a laser beam on the right frequency could direct them to a pinpoint hit—say, right into the vest of a man standing in the open, as Swayne had done on the last mission to the Middle East.

Night Runner had his setup. He raised his rifle, reading the heads-up display in his scope. He swept the sky in a regular pattern, assuming that the aircraft would have been launched from Diego Garcia in the Indian Ocean.

Finally, he saw in his sight what he was looking for, a sparkle of light that indicated an electronic emission. The laser-guided bomb was sending back video images to the mother ship. Although radar might not pick up the aircraft, anybody with a receiver like the one in Night Runner's rifle scope could pick it up, translate it, and using the computer set in the PDA, capture the bomb.

Night Runner centered the sparkle in his scope. He

turned on his laser beam. Nothing. He painted the area around the sparkle. Still nothing.

He concentrated, sweeping the spot in the sky until he got a response, a flash of recognition, as if somebody were flashing a spotlight at him from five miles up.

The receiver in the nose of the bomb had picked up his laser beam. It had redirected its course to fly down his laser beam directly at the palace.

Night Runner quickly touched the keys on his PDA, sending a signal to the bomb, changing its capture frequency to match that in the laser beam of his scope so control could not be taken from him by the onboard computers in the plane.

He could only guess what was going on at the controls of the bomber. The bombardier had been watching his LGB fly down the chute toward a fire, which somehow had erupted outside the mosque. But now, it had suddenly flown out of control. It was now aimed at a different target in the city. He would be trying to abort the mission, jabbing at buttons to get the self-destruct feature to detonate the bomb in the air.

But the plane had lost control. The bomb now belonged to two forces: a Force Recon Marine and gravity.

Night Runner kept his aim sure, hoping he could direct the LGB so radically off course.

IN THE TACTICAL Operations Center, Zavello had a satellite feed right to his station.

He had told himself he would not watch what the political leaders of this country were going to do to one of his Marines.

He had long ago stopped yelling for Swayne to answer. He had already told the Administration that communications had been cut. He was more concerned that the Iranians had captured his man than whether he was going to get his ass chewed by the President.

When the National Security Adviser had continued to nag at him, Zavello had shut him up with a one-eyed glance. "The best you can hope for now is that the Iranians have those Marines. And they're taking them to the mosque. The only way you're going to be lucky is if that entire Force Recon Team gets wiped out when that bomb hits. If not, you'll have an awful lot to answer for. Because it now looks like they have four Marines instead of one."

"Your head is going to roll," the President's adviser had said.

"See you at the guillotine," Zavello had said with a snarl.

But now both of them had become as captivated as that laser-guided bomb.

He knew damned well what was happening. It gave him a great sense of relief that his men were not dead. At least one of them had the wherewithal and the wits to capture that laser-guided bomb. They might not be talking to him over the radio, but he knew they were alive: Nobody in the world could pull off a stunt like that except perhaps Swayne. Or his sergeant, Night Runner.

Zavello switched to a radio band so he could eavesdrop on the Air Force transmissions. It gave him a laughing fit to hear the screeching going on back and forth among the boys in blue. Somebody had told the pilots that their bomb could hit a residential neighborhood. Somebody was screaming for the bomb to be blown up in flight.

The pilots were screaming back that they no longer had control over the bomb. It had been taken off their frequencies. It was nothing more now than a hunk of explosive wrapped in metal casing falling to the ground.

Zavello knew better. Somebody out there in the Middle East was making one hell of a big decision. With everything else now out of control, he hoped that that one person did have all the buttons at his fingertips. And that he knew what he was doing.

NIGHT RUNNER SWITCHED off his scope, cutting the beam, letting the bomb fall in a ballistic mode. It would stay on it momentarily. Until he reversed his rifle and pointed the laser at the top of a massive gazebo roof in the garden below him. Then he turned it back on, hoping the signal was strong and readable from the position of the hurtling bomb.

He watched the screen of his hand-held computer, waiting for the capture. Without that, that bomb would fall where gravity let it. It could strike on the palace grounds. Might land half a mile away and kill a few hundred people.

He watched the screen. He needed to capture it soon. He wiggled the laser spot on the gazebo like wiggling a worm on a hook in a trout pond. The course correction that he was going to ask this missile to make—

There!

He had a capture. Slowly, Night Runner began moving the laser spot. Occasionally, he would lose it, when it was diffused in the foliage. Then he would find a hard target and plaster the dot on the side of a building until the bomb was recaptured.

In his head, the countdown continued. In his mind, he still had too great a distance to move that bomb. The airport was at least five miles away. If he could make course corrections quickly enough, the bomb might be able to fly. Most likely, this was not going to work. There was no way that bomb was going to change direction by five miles in the minute-plus of free-fall time that remained.

Nevertheless, Night Runner kept working on the problem. At least he had gotten the thing to fly away from the palace. At least it could not take out him and the rest of the team.

He moved the spot as quickly as he could across the landscape. As the bomb fell closer to earth, the adjustment distance that he could get out of it became less.

He moved the beam, checked the screen, got the capture, moved again.

Each time, he had to wait longer and longer for the capture. Unless he moved it a shorter and shorter distance, which gave the same result.

Night Runner understood finally, when he had perhaps thirty seconds left in the free fall of the bomb, that he was not going to make the parking lot on the far end of the airport where Azzan's jet had been parked. The best he could hope for was the airstrip itself, a mile away. But at least it was a mile farther from the palace.

Finally, he found the navigation marker at the end of the airstrip. He held the dot there, hoping for the capture. It did not come. He waved the dot around, moving it back to a shack on the hillside below the airport. Got the capture. Moved until the navigation device lost it. Got it back. Lost it.

A huge flash wiped out his scope.

Night Runner did not spend any time worrying about what damage might have been done at the airfield. He might have destroyed the navigation device. Or not. He might have missed altogether, the bomb knocking out an empty, useless shack.

No matter. He needed to get to Friel. He ran down the stairwell into the ballroom. There he found the sergeant standing in the broken glass, his feet bleeding. Greiner stood beside Friel. In one hand, he held his survival knife, which he'd used to cut the ropes that held Friel to the chair. In the other hand, he held out a piece of cloth.

Night Runner recognized it as one of the wraps taken

from the Iranian women. Friel wasn't about to put on a dress.

Friel had other things on his mind besides getting decent. Night Runner could see the intent in even the dim light of the ballroom. Friel was going to get even.

The battered face revealed nothing but hatred.

He was holding a rifle, one of the AK-47's that had belonged to the terrorists.

Night Runner knelt, pulling off his pack.

"I have some socks. A clean shirt," he said.

Friel did not reply.

"Gunny," Greiner said, dropping the woman's wrap.

"I see." Night Runner saw the muzzle of the rifle twitch, then begin to rise toward him.

"You want me to—"

"I want you to stay out of this," said Night Runner. "No matter what happens, don't butt in, understand?"

"Gunny?"

"Understand?"

"Yes, Gunny." Greiner took a step backward. He lowered his knife, but pulled at the sling of his rifle. The gunny might know what he was doing, trying to deal with a crazy man, but Greiner wasn't about to take a chance. If Friel opened up at Night Runner, he, Greiner, was going to take out Friel.

SWAYNE CAME AWAKE realizing that he'd lost consciousness. He thought he'd heard an explosion, but couldn't be sure.

Feeling stabs of pain and difficulty in breathing, he rolled onto his side.

At first he thought he was dreaming. But no, he saw the man with the rifle raising it toward another man.

He recognized the two of them and tried to call out, but managed little better than a squeak. He knew he had so little breath he wouldn't sound like himself, even if he could be heard.

He felt around himself and came up with what he wanted. His carbine. It took a huge physical effort to bring it to bear on the window, and an even greater effort to will himself to lay the sight on the side of Friel's head.

At the edge of his scope, he saw the focus in Greiner's eyes, and knew that if he failed to kill Friel, the new guy would do it.

Suddenly, he realized that Azzan had defeated him once more. First in the desert, then here, then by escaping.

Somehow the terrorist had maneuvered the Force Recon Marines into a position of killing each other. Certainly, he'd not done it by design, but the result would be the same.

Friel, who'd been thrown to the enemy by a foolish act of Night Runner, now held a rifle on the gunny, and looked as if he'd gone mad enough to kill his NCO. Either Greiner or Swayne would kill Friel in return. Maybe Friel would get Greiner too. Leaving Swayne to lie here helpless. He'd either bleed to death or drown in his own blood or be captured by the Ayatollah's Army.

Swayne felt a deep shame. He'd let down his men by not being the kind of officer they'd needed. His grandfather, Jamison Swayne, had been right all along.

He wasn't cut out to be a soldier after all.

He'd lost his nerve. The only way to get back his resolve now was to kill his own man.

He felt the fuzziness closing in on the edges of his vision. *Damn!* He'd been outsmarted by the terrorist, the first soldier he'd ever known to beat him at his own game on the field of brainpower.

The slack came out of his trigger.

Too late.

The ballroom of the palace erupted in gunfire.

The last Swayne saw was the strobe lighting of the

ballroom caused by the AK-47 going off on full automatic in Friel's hands.

He squeezed off a long burst, but his vision had blinked out and he didn't even know whether he'd hit anything.

EPILOGUE

FOR NINA CHASE, the whole trip to Iran was a bust. She never even got out of Tehran, although she'd had a personal invitation from Azzan to visit Mashhad.

She waved her invitation in the bureaucrat's face, but all she got was: "The holy city has been closed due to the unfortunate intervention by the Great Satan America in the affairs of the Holy Revolutionary Government of Iran."

She didn't even argue. Somehow, in her last adventure, the trip into Kosovo that now seemed so long ago, the fire in her belly had been extinguished.

All she wanted now was to get back to the States. Relax. Call Jack Swayne for the thousandth time in the last week. He must have been out on one of his missions.

She hoped he'd get back in one piece. She had needs.

SWAYNE HADN'T BEEN able to satisfy any of Nina's needs for a long time. He'd been put on medical leave to recover physically, which didn't take long. But he needed to be restored in the mental department as well.

After six weeks, he finally relented and returned a call. They met at a retreat in the Cascades east of Seattle. She was gentle with him at first. But in the end, she achieved what she'd gone after.

Afterward, he began to believe for the first time that he could go back to duty in Force Recon.

He wasn't sure what kind of team he'd have to work with. But he knew he'd be willing to try to work with whatever he found.

NIGHT RUNNER AT last had found bravery. Both on the mountain in Montana and in the palace in Mashhad. In one case, facing a grizzly. In the other case, facing an enraged marine.

In Montana, he had artificially put himself into harm's way to prove his bravery to himself. The grizzly had stood in place a long time, trying to decide what to make of the unusual situation of a man who smelled both like a fish and a freshly wounded animal.

The animal leaned forward and dropped to all fours. Approaching Night Runner, it pushed against his right knee as it tested the scent of fish. Night Runner felt himself tremble all over. He was sorry he'd allowed this situation to happen. He gripped the knife in a sweaty palm.

The bear lapped his leg once and snorted.

"I understand, my brother. I'm sorry to do this to you. I ask you to leave me here unharmed. If you attack me, I will fight back. But if you leave, I will go away, never to bother you again."

The bear decided the taste of fish did not mingle well with a man's sweat. It turned and ambled into the forest, leaving Night Runner alone with his stupidity.

In Iran, Night Runner had faced a more dangerous situation, a man obsessed with the idea of killing him. He could see in the dim light that Friel had been tortured. He saw marks from cigarette burns. He saw other burn marks that might have come from electrical sparks.

And he saw the look in Friel's eyes.

"I understand, my brother. I'm sorry I did this to you."

That was all he said. He made no threat, as with the bear. As on that night in Montana, he had a weapon, the rifle he held by his side. He had no intention of using it. He did not want to die, but he would not kill Friel to save his own life. He'd already killed something in the man. He saw in the eyes that something had died. Something more vital than a life. His spirit.

FRIEL HAD WAITED for the moment. He'd seethed for too long. Officers and gunnery sergeants. Always acting superior. But they were supposed to look out for their men, not leave them in the desert to be kidnapped by terrorists.

He had every intention of killing Night Runner. The terrorists had done things to him. Not just the things that left visible scars. Other things. Things he could never admit to, not even to a shrink.

Now the object of his hatred stood there. He waited for the gunny to make his move, to raise his gun. He'd take out the chief, then the new guy, who'd already showed his hand.

Then Night Runner said the words he'd never expected to hear. "My brother." Night Runner said he was sorry, which he sure as hell ought to be. After he'd called him his brother.

All the hatred drained as if a spigot had opened in his gut. Friel actually looked down to see if he could see it leaking onto the floor to pool beside his bloody feet.

Then he heard it. The sound of squealing glass.

Everything happened at once.

Night Runner dived.

Friel fired the AK-47 on full auto.

He saw the figure splattered hard with maybe twenty-eight of the thirty rounds in the clip—he'd not lost his shooting touch.

He smiled unaware of Swayne's slugs spattering the palace walls outside.

Finally, he was even. Finally, he'd gotten his freaking revenge.

Mindless of his own bleeding feet, he crossed the ball-room. Outside on the patio lying in a puddle was a man draped in freaking sheets. Friel cocked his head to be sure of who it was.

Yes. Azzan.

"Bastid."

GREINER WAS CONFUSED for a long while. First, the corporal pulling down on the gunny. Then, the gunny leaping at Greiner as Friel's gun went off, preventing him from killing the guy he thought was trying to kill the gunny.

Finally, he got it sorted out.

But he didn't have much time to enjoy that things had turned out mostly okay. There was the captain lying shot outside. All the commotion at the palace was going to draw a lot of attention once the bombings got sorted out.

Gunny put him to work right away, and he didn't have time to get his mind right for a while.

He had to drive the motorcycle. First, ferrying Friel out of the city to hide out in the culvert. Then, returning to pick up the captain and the gunny. Night Runner held the captain between them as they got clear of the last check-point and met a helicopter. It took Swayne away imme-diately.

While Night Runner and he went back for Friel.

Night Runner insisted on dressing the women at the culvert. He gave them solvent to clean off the bad-ass duct tape, and cut the hobbles off their ankles too.

The first rays of dawn had already begun to light up the horizon when they'd finally double-timed it to an LZ for a second helicopter that took them clear of Iran.

All the way out of the country, Friel kept murmuring:

"Goddamned Iran. I ain't never coming back to this godforsaken place."

Greiner stared at Friel. He was, he decided, certifiably nuts. But Friel clapped him on the back. For the first time since he'd known him, in a friendly way.

"I hope the hell you stick with us, Grinder. We been needing a good man like you for a helluva long time."

Greiner didn't need Friel telling him he'd won his spot on the Spartans. He knew he'd done his job like a pro.

Still, it felt good. Considering the source.

James V. Smith
Force Recon
series

Count your losses—take no prisoners.

Force Recon	0-425-16975-8
Death Wind	0-425-17406-9
The Butcher's Bill	0-425-17814-5

**Available wherever books are sold or to order call
1-800-788-6262**

RULES OF ENGAGEMENT
Gordon Kent
0-425-17858-7

He watched helplessly as his father's fighter plane was shot down by Iranians in the skies above the Persian Gulf. Now, Naval Intelligence officer Alan Craik is taking on the investigation, going outside of the rules, and heading straight toward a showdown with a man within his own ranks-an American turned traitor and executioner...

"An impressive debut."—*Kirkus Review*

"The best military thriller in years..."
—Patrick Davis

PENGUIN PUTNAM INC.
Online

Your Internet gateway to a virtual environment with
hundreds of entertaining and enlightening books
from Penguin Putnam Inc.

*While you're there, get the latest buzz on
the best authors and books around—*

Tom Clancy, Patricia Cornwell, W.E.B. Griffin,
Nora Roberts, William Gibson, Robin Cook,
Brian Jacques, Catherine Coulter, Stephen King,
Ken Follett, Terry McMillan, and many more!

**Penguin Putnam Online is located at
http://www.penguinputnam.com**

PENGUIN PUTNAM NEWS

Every month you'll get an inside look at our upcom-
ing books and new features on our site. This is an
ongoing effort to provide you with the most
up-to-date information about
our books and authors.

**Subscribe to Penguin Putnam News at
http://www.penguinputnam.com/newsletters**